ALICE
SHARPE

MULTIPLES
MYSTERY

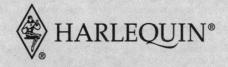

HARLEQUIN®

TORONTO • NEW YORK • LONDON
AMSTERDAM • PARIS • SYDNEY • HAMBURG
STOCKHOLM • ATHENS • TOKYO • MILAN • MADRID
PRAGUE • WARSAW • BUDAPEST • AUCKLAND

This book is dedicated to mothers everywhere.

Recycling programs
for this product may
not exist in your area.

ISBN-13: 978-0-373-88898-6
ISBN-10:   0-373-88898-8

MULTIPLES MYSTERY

"Zac, I don't know what I'd do without you."

He smiled, then reached down to help her get off the low futon. She was spooked by the events of the evening and his warm hand just made her feel better. "You're shaking."

"It's been a very long past few days." She fought the urge to ask him to stay, but she had no right. He was already doing more than he probably should.

"I'll swing by later, check in on you and the girls. Keep the doors locked."

"Okay," she said as a warm tear slid down her face.

He caught it on his fingertip. "Hey, I thought you didn't cry."

"I don't. It's the hormones. I have too many of them and they're running amok."

And then he dipped his head, kissed her cheek.

She stood looking after him, her fingers against the place where his lips had touched. Beneath the layer of fear kindled by Zac's warnings, another feeling tried to break through.

She pushed it away....

ABOUT THE AUTHOR

Alice Sharpe met her husband-to-be on a cold, foggy beach in Northern California. One year later they were married. Their union has survived the rearing of two children, a handful of earthquakes registering over 6.5, numerous cats and a few special dogs, the latest of which is a yellow Lab named Annie Rose. Alice and her husband now live in a small rural town in Oregon, where she devotes the majority of her time to pursuing her second love, writing.

Alice loves to hear from readers. You can write her at P.O. Box 755, Brownsville, OR 97327. SASE for reply is appreciated.

Books by Alice Sharpe

HARLEQUIN INTRIGUE
746—FOR THE SAKE OF THEIR BABY
823—UNDERCOVER BABIES
923—MY SISTER, MYSELF*
929—DUPLICATE DAUGHTER*
1022—ROYAL HEIR
1051—AVENGING ANGEL
1076—THE LAWMAN'S SECRET SON**
1082—BODYGUARD FATHER**
1124—MULTIPLES MYSTERY

*Dead Ringer
**Skye Brother Babies

CAST OF CHARACTERS

Olivia Capri—She's just given birth to four beautiful baby girls. Life should be brimming with hope, but the husband Olivia married after a whirlwind romance is missing. Where is he?

Zac Bishop—He's loved Olivia from afar for more years than he can remember. His goal: make her love him back. First he'll have to do everything he can to keep her alive.

Anthony Capri—A larger-than-life man with a mysterious past. Have his actions set in motion a chain of events that will jeopardize the lives of his wife and babies?

Faith Bishop—Zac's sister, Olivia's best friend, the quads' unofficial nanny. A small woman with a big heart and a vital role to play.

Brad Makko—He's the brother-in-law Olivia never knew existed. His revelations about his brother are terrifying.

Grant and Hugh Robinson—These aging brothers are furious Anthony Capri duped them and pretty sure Olivia knows all about it. How far will they take revenge?

"The Gamblers"—A misfit trio out to collect what's owed to them, no matter which innocent gets in the way.

"Twitch"—Is he a harmless hanger-on, a hired gun or a man with a secret agenda?

Juliet, Sandy, Megan and Tabitha Hart—Olivia's mother and sisters, the women she depends on.

Juliet, Brianna, Jillian and Antoinette Capri—The newborns Olivia and Zac will die to protect.

Chapter One

Olivia Capri gingerly swung her legs over the edge of the hospital bed and sat there a moment, fighting a wave of dizziness. Not bad and to be expected after two months of bed rest. She breathed deeply a few times, taking in the Seattle skyline through her window, preparing herself for the next move, the one onto her feet.

Where was Anthony? Why hadn't he come? He'd been acting so odd lately, so distant...

She could not lie in that bed another moment. She'd been stuck in it for what seemed forever, a fate she'd suffered with good grace as every moment the babies stayed inside her body where they belonged, the better their chances of survival once they were born. But they were out now, all four of them, declared amazingly healthy considering they were premature, and tucked away in the Special Care Nursery.

She put her weight on her feet and stood slowly.

The incision from the C-section made itself known and she winced, but it wasn't that bad. She could handle it.

A sound at the door thundered in her anxious brain and she steadied herself by grabbing the bed rail. She looked up in time to find Faith crossing the threshold.

"What are you doing?" Faith said.

Olivia's heart plummeted. She loved Faith like a sister, but hers wasn't the face Olivia hoped to see.

"I'm going to go find my babies and then I'm going to go find my husband." Her voice sounded kind of wavery, a surprise. "Unless maybe you've heard from him," she added hopefully.

"Not a peep," Faith said, closing the space between them in three steps. She gently took Olivia's arm and said, "Get back in bed, you nut."

"Faith, I'm warning you—"

"Not even you can go through what you've gone through today and stagger on down the hall by yourself. I'll get the nurse. Just get in bed and wait for a wheelchair."

"The nurse won't let me go until the doctor checks me over, and the doctor is in surgery."

"Get in bed," Faith said in her stern, brook-no-nonsense voice. She might be a petite woman—five-feet, almost nothing to Olivia's five-feet-seven—but over a lifetime Olivia had learned when to take her friend seriously. She sat back on the mattress.

"I'm going crazy," she said, "and my babies are all alone—"

"Hardly. Your mom and two of your sisters are down there driving the nurses wacko. When the two of us show up and Anthony arrives, we'll outnumber the staff."

"Don't even say his name," Olivia grumbled.

Faith pushed a wavy strand of wheat-colored hair behind her ear and said, "He'll come. Something must have happened. Traffic, maybe. An accident. A fender bender."

"A fender bender that killed his cell phone? You know he doesn't go anywhere without that thing."

Faith nodded. "I know."

"He'd better be dead or I'm going to kill him."

Faith shook her head. "You don't mean that."

Olivia did the unthinkable. She burst into tears.

Faith enfolded her in a hug and rocked her. "Sweetie, you're scared." She paused for a second before adding, "I talked to Zac today. He's coming by later, we'll get him to go look for Anthony."

"I can't bother Zac," Olivia blubbered against Faith's shoulder. "He's a big-city cop now. Besides, he hates me."

"He doesn't hate you."

"I told him I was never going to talk to him again."

"He's my brother. I tell him that every two weeks."

"And I don't cry. You know I don't cry."

"I know. Come on, calm down, all these raging hormones are to be expected. Hey, I know something that will cheer you up. I have baby pictures. Want to see? They're on my cell phone."

"Of course I want to see," Olivia said, accepting a wad of tissue from Faith and wiping her eyes. She took a few deep breaths. Faith helped her settle back on the mattress and pull a lightweight blanket over her bare legs.

Olivia sighed. *Back in bed where she started.*

What she wouldn't give to gather up her new family and go home to Westerly. How was that for irony? She'd spent twenty-seven years trying to get out of the place and now all she wanted was to get back.

Perching lightly on the edge of the mattress, Faith fiddled with the phone. "Okay, here we go. I took them in order so you'd know who's who."

The tiny screen filled with the image of a very pink baby with its eyes squeezed shut. Olivia had named her babies weeks before, deciding on who got which name based solely on birth order. She'd asked Anthony what he thought and he'd agreed that was fine with him.

Had he looked bored with the subject?

No, she couldn't think like that. It wasn't fair.

"Jillian," she whispered, her eyes brimming with new tears.

"She's the biggest at four pounds, six ounces," Faith said. "Look, she has your hair."

"They all have my hair," Olivia said lovingly.

"Think how family pictures are going to look," Faith said. "You and the girls with long, black hair, and Anthony with a blond buzz cut."

Olivia swallowed a lump as she scrolled down to the next photo. Another baby, not quite as pink, face not so scrunched. Olivia was glad to see the little wristbands each child wore—it was a fear of hers that she'd mix her children up, call them by the wrong name… She wondered if she'd ever feel secure enough to take the bracelets off.

"That's Brianna," Faith said.

"Three pounds, eight ounces, right?"

"You heard the doctor?"

"Yes." A wave of frustration surged through her body. "Where's my buzzer? I want to talk to that nurse—"

"Look at the rest of the pictures first. Then I'll go find a wheelchair and we'll break you out of this joint."

"What would I do without you?" Olivia asked, glancing up at her friend.

"Founder on the rocks of disaster?"

Olivia smiled as she moved on to the next baby. This little doll looked like her sister, Brianna. The truth was, wearing just diapers and little stocking caps, they all looked more or less alike. Time would change that—maybe. No one was sure right now if they were all identical or two sets of twins or triplets and a single—there was no easy way to tell.

"And this is Juliet, named after your mother," Faith said. "Look at her little nose."

"They all have little noses and rosebud mouths," Olivia murmured. They were all exquisite.

"And last but not least, Antoinette," Faith said.

"Named after her father," Olivia said, touching the two-inch screen with a fingertip.

They were so impossibly defenseless. They would need time and care to catch up to their full-term peers, time and care to grow strong and robust, and it would be up to her to see they got it.

Where did that thought come from? Anthony would show up. Wouldn't he?

A jolt of white-hot anger cut through her worry. Anthony should be with the babies right now, watching over them when she couldn't, caring about what happened to them, instead of leaving it all to Olivia's family and friends.

Shame immediately followed the anger. What if he really was lying hurt and battered somewhere? What if he'd tried to come? What if someone had attacked him, robbed him, left him to die—what kind of beast was she?

The door opened again and both women tensed, but it wasn't Anthony who walked into the room. Zachary Bishop, Faith's brother, looked from one anxious face to the other and stopped dead in his tracks. "If this isn't a good time—"

"Come on in, Zac," Faith said as she slipped off the bed. His smile of greeting for his sister faded as his gaze sought out and held Olivia's.

Unlike petite Faith, Zac was tall and rangy, with straight brown hair cut shorter than usual, intense blue eyes and a broken nose that had healed crooked in an interesting way. A faded scar ran diagonally across his chin and another bisected his left eyebrow, both remnants of a drunken brawl he broke up his first year as a Deputy Sheriff back in Westerly.

But he wasn't a deputy anymore. He was a Seattle cop, a position he had taken while she and Anthony had been on their honeymoon. Still, she'd be willing to bet he was the same old Zac underneath the fancy new suit, a man of swift action and few words.

"How's the new mother?" he asked, and to her relief, his voice sounded the way it always had.

Maybe they could put the past behind them and be friends again.

"The truth? I'm going a little stir-crazy."

He produced a quartet of pink roses from behind his back and handed them to her.

The simple message of the flowers touched her more than the huge bouquets that lined the shelf, sent by everyone she knew and some people she didn't. "One for each baby," she said softly, fingering the blushed petals. Meeting his gaze again, she said, "Thank you, Zac."

He nodded.

"Have you seen them?"

"Briefly. I had to wave a badge to get into the place. Security is tight. They're cute but kind of tiny, aren't they?"

"They'll grow," Faith said.

Zac nodded. No one spoke for several seconds. In the past, the three of them had talked over the top of each other half the time. To fill the void, Olivia said, "How do you like your new job?"

"It keeps me busy," he said, stuffing his hands in his pockets, jingling keys or loose change.

"How about living in Seattle?"

He shrugged. "It has its moments."

Faith said, "My brother, the big talker."

"Well I think it must be very exciting," Olivia

said. "Lots more happening here than in Westerly. Are you on a big case?"

"Actually, things are in flux."

"What does that mean?" Faith asked.

"It means things are in flux."

"Zac!"

A fond smile lifted the corners of his mouth as he stared at Faith. "You haven't changed a bit since you were ten years old." With a shift of gaze to Olivia, he added, "Neither have you. You've both always been too nosey for your own good."

"You're one to talk," Olivia said softly, but he apparently heard her and again their eyes met.

"Touché," he said. "Okay, you guys win. I'll talk on the condition that what I say stays in this room for now."

Zac groaned as Faith mimed zipping her lips. He stared them each in the eye and said, "Sheriff Knotts got caught stealing marijuana from the evidence room."

Both women blinked before Olivia said, "Our Sheriff Knotts? Bobby Knotts of Westerly?"

"The very one."

"How does a crooked sheriff in Westerly tie in to your job in Seattle?" Faith demanded.

"Knotts has been asked to resign immediately pending criminal investigation. Half the sheriff's department is implicated. Since I left some time ago, it's been decided I'm the one guy who knows the ropes and isn't tainted by Knotts."

"Dad is going to be dancing in the streets," Faith said. "You're moving back to Westerly!"

Zac nodded.

"That's great," Faith gushed.

He held up one hand. "I haven't accepted yet. I don't know if I want to be interim sheriff. I'm not sure I want to move back to Westerly." He glanced at the flowers in Olivia's hands and turned to his sister. "Would you mind finding a vase for the flowers?"

"You're getting rid of me. No, I don't mind. Back in a moment."

"Don't forget to steal a wheelchair," Olivia called after her.

Faith nodded, then cast her brother a quick look. "I need to talk to you before you leave."

Olivia looked Zac over as he stared after his sister. At thirty-five, he appeared to be in his prime, the boyish mannerisms gone, replaced with easy sophistication. However, under that big-city gray suit she knew beat the heart of a small-town lawman, a man who knew his place in the scheme of the universe. Not for the first time, she wondered what had driven him to leave Westerly.

It couldn't have been their fight. Something like

that wasn't important enough to drive a man away from his family and friends and his career.

As if attuned to the direction of her thoughts, he looked down at his feet, then into her eyes. "I wanted a minute alone to apologize to you, Olivia."

No need to ask for what.

"I shouldn't have spoken to you like I did. I had no right."

"No, you didn't," she said. "And on my wedding day, too, Zac. That was just plain mean."

"Yeah. Anyway, I've always thought of you as a little sister, like Faith, but you aren't."

"No, I'm not. You telling me I absolutely could not marry Anthony Capri was totally out of place. Frankly, even if you'd been my brother it would have been going too far."

"I know that now."

"You really upset me."

"I'm sorry. Am I forgiven?"

She stared at him a second, then smiled. "Of course you're forgiven." She'd missed him. She was ready to let that unfortunate day go. Like Faith, Zac was as good as family, and family had to forgive and forget, otherwise there'd be no one to spend holidays with. "Are you really thinking about taking the sheriff's job and coming back to Westerly?"

"That depends on you," he said.

She furrowed her brow. "Me?"

"And Anthony. I wouldn't want to make either of you uncomfortable."

She said, "I've never told Anthony what you said about him that day, Zac. What would that have accomplished? You take the job if you want, too. I think Westerly is big enough for all three of us."

He nodded once. "Fair enough. So, do you know what Faith wants to talk to me about?" He glanced around the room before adding, "Where is Anthony anyway?"

"That's what she wants to talk to you about," Olivia said, leaning forward to reach the water glass. She'd pushed the tray too far away, however.

Apparently taking pity on her feeble attempts, Zac handed it over with questions burning in his eyes. She gave him the flowers and he set them on the tray. "Did he leave already?"

She wanted to say, *Yes, he left a few minutes ago. He's the most devoted husband on the planet. You were totally wrong about him.*

"He didn't come," she admitted, busying herself taking sips of ice water.

"He didn't come?" Zac repeated, stepping closer. "What do you mean?"

"Just what I said. I don't know why. I'm worried sick, of course, but he didn't come or call or…anything."

"Maybe he's been in an accident."

"I thought of that. Faith said we should ask you to do something, but I don't want to be a bother."

He took the water glass from her hands and set it back on the tray next to the flowers, then hitched his hands on his waist and stared down at her. "When was the last time you saw him or talked to him?"

"The day before yesterday."

"And he knew about today's scheduled births?"

"Yes."

"Did he plan to be here?"

"Yes. Of course."

"Could he have forgotten?"

"I don't see how, though I know he's in the middle of a deal—"

"Like the one he drummed up in Westerly? What was it, a chain of snowboard and ski shops? He talked the Robinson brothers into investing, right?"

"He put in money of his own, too," she said. "He's quite wealthy." She didn't know why she added that last part, except that Zac looked so smug.

"Must be that Harvard education of his."

"Or the fact that he invested in Midas Touch Computers before anyone else did. Jealous?"

He held up both hands as though backing off. "Sorry. You have to admit, though, the man is larger than life. Navy pilot, Super Bowl champion… He's done it all."

Zac could just not help himself. When it came to

Anthony's exploits, give Zac enough rope and he'd hang himself. Determined to keep the peace of their newly repaired friendship, she said, "Yes, he has." Actually, after weeks of misgivings and a morning spent cursing his absence, it almost felt good to defend her husband. Oh, God, maybe he really was hurt and she was being a raging, selfish bitch.

"I see," Zac said, and by the tone of his voice, he saw a lot more than Olivia was comfortable with.

"I know he wanted to be here," she insisted. *Liar. Tell him the truth. Tell him you think what really happened is your husband got cold feet and ran away, that he was willing to risk millions in investment dollars rather than face you and four babies.*

Zac said, "I heard you guys are building a house out by the point."

"Yes."

"Is that where he's been living since you started bed rest here?"

"No, he stayed in my old place in town in order to hurry the contractors along so we could take the babies home as soon as possible."

"When will that be?"

"Not long. The doctor wants them here until they each reach four pounds. Two were born over four pounds and two aren't far away. But they'll probably lose a little weight before bulking back up, so it's kind of a day by day thing."

"Where did he stay when he wasn't in Westerly?"

"He has a suite at the Marina Inn here in Seattle."

"The Marina Inn. Nothing but the best, huh?" He raised a hand again and shook his head. "Sorry."

"You just can't help yourself."

"I'm trying. Okay, that's enough to start. I'll drive over to the hotel. Try not to worry, I'm sure something unexpected came up." He stared deep into her eyes, then he smiled the old familiar Zac smile.

She caught his hand. "You'll come back? You'll tell me what's wrong even if it's—unpleasant?"

"What do you mean 'unpleasant'?"

"Like he's hurt or… I don't know. Missing, maybe."

"I'll tell you whatever I find out." He stared at her a moment longer, and then he leaned down and brushed her forehead with his lips.

"I've always valued our friendship," she mumbled as their eyes met.

"I know," he said softly, and then he was gone.

ZAC FOUND FAITH by the nurses station, holding a slender vase in one hand and gripping the countertop with the other. She was talking to a nurse on the other side. The colorful smock the nurse wore looked a lot cheerier than either woman's expression.

Faith shook her head as he joined her. "It's no use, rules are rules. Olivia is going to have to wait."

Zac turned to the nurse. "Have a heart."

"As I told this lady," the nurse explained patiently, "we're waiting for Mrs. Capri's doctor to give the okay. He's been called into emergency surgery. When he has time, I'm sure he'll release her."

"She's a new mom. There's no real reason for her to have to wait. She's a very fit young woman who's been athletic her whole life. Let her call the shots of what she can and can't do."

"Not without—"

"I mean, how would it sound," Zac mused, "if the press got wind that the new mother of quads couldn't see them?"

The nurse's eyebrows rose. "Maybe you have a point," she said. "It doesn't do to be a slave to rules."

"I agree with you," Zac said with a smile.

"I'll go take her vitals and if everything checks out, I'll get a wheelchair."

"Excellent," Zac said. "Thanks."

He and Faith watched the woman hustle down the corridor toward Olivia's room, snagging a vitals cart as she passed one. Faith said, "That was smooth."

"Maybe she could sense I was ready to shoot her if she didn't cooperate."

Faith grinned. She was short and willowy with a pale complexion and pretty, girl-next-door looks— the opposite of Olivia, who was tall and graceful with dark, exotic beauty. Faith was a teacher by trade, patient and good-tempered by nature, a homebody. Olivia could be impulsive and restless. Faith dated regularly, though she'd yet to find the love of her life. Olivia kept men at arm's length, always too busy planning for the day she could strike out and see the world. That is, that's what she'd been like before Anthony Capri came along.

"Is Juliet Hart still in with the babies?" he asked.

"No, I just saw her. She left Olivia's sisters to look after things while she arranges a press conference. She wants to make sure the babies hit the state news before Olivia takes them back to Westerly. I think she's afraid they'll fade into obscurity before she gets her moment in the sun as the grandmother of the state's newest quadruplets."

"I wanted to ask her if she's heard from Anthony."

"She hasn't, I asked. Olivia told you about him?"

"That he didn't come for the births? That he left her here alone?" A knot worked in his jaw as he reined in his temper and said, "She's convinced he's had an accident or some kind of unavoidable delay."

"Is she?"

"Isn't she?"

Faith shrugged. "I'm not sure." She studied his face for a second before adding, "I'm glad you came, Zac. I kind of thought you might show up before, while she was stuck in here—"

"I didn't want to get in the way," he said quickly. "Stay close to her, will you?"

"I'm on leave from the school for the rest of the spring semester, and then I have all summer. I'm not going anywhere."

"She's going to need help."

"She'll get it. I'll be her unofficial nanny. The rest of Westerly is behind her and Anthony."

"They've known Olivia forever," Zac said. "She does the bookkeeping for half of the small businesses in town."

"And everyone likes Anthony," Faith said, "even though he's a newcomer. Plus, you know, Anthony is rolling in dough. Olivia can afford to quit work and hire help."

He had nothing to say to that. It was true. Anthony could give Olivia the life she wanted. Travel, excitement, adventure. Only right now, all she wanted was his presence. "I have an appointment later that I can't break. Between now and then I'll do what I can to track down the new daddy. Call me if he shows up here."

Faith's small hand wrapped around his forearm. "Zac, Olivia's gut is telling her Anthony isn't happy about becoming a father. I think she's worried he's run out on her."

"I'm sorry to hear that," Zac said, though he wasn't surprised. The Anthony Capris of the world liked to be the center of attention. Being relegated to second fiddle behind a beautiful wife and four adorable babies wouldn't appeal to him. "Maybe he just got new-dad jitters. I'll try to find him and talk some sense into him."

Faith bit her bottom lip, something she often did when she wasn't sure if she wanted to say something or not. She obviously decided to go for it. "There's something else. Grant Robinson is making noise. He says Anthony hasn't been returning calls. Hugh is mad as a hornet, too, but you know Grant, he's the one who runs around making threats. You know what a hothead he can be."

"Great," Zac said. "If I take the sheriff job, I'll inherit the Robinson brothers. Well, one thing at a time. First I find Anthony."

"Hurry," Faith said. "I didn't tell Olivia this, but I called the hotel, you know, to get someone to knock on his door in case Anthony, well, you know, overslept or got sick or something."

"And?"

"They couldn't find his reservation. I didn't have time to go through the whole process of them figuring out what they'd done wrong, but Zac, I have a bad feeling about this."

Chapter Two

Anthony Capri hadn't been missing long enough to tap official channels. For that matter, he wasn't missing at all. He just hadn't shown up where he damn well should have been.

Why? How does a man forget such a thing as his wife giving birth to quadruplets? Everyone from Westerly to Seattle knew about it!

That left an accident or foul play. Zac didn't like the man, that was true. Capri was a natural born salesman, glib and charming, self-deprecating and able to relate to anyone. That, in Zac's book, made him as slick as a shucked oyster, the kind of guy who could talk a snake into buying socks. Zac just plain didn't trust him.

But Olivia did, and right now, that was all that mattered.

The month of May could be beautiful in Seattle and today was one of the better examples. Fluffy white clouds, crystal blue skies, the distant peak of

Mt. Rainier—the city looked like one of the post-cards for sale down at Pike Place Market.

All that said, it was still a sprawling city with major traffic issues and he wasn't a sprawling city kind of guy. Olivia said it was okay with her if he moved back. Anthony, even if he wasn't dead or halfway across the country, wouldn't care one way or another. That meant it was up to him and he wasn't sure he could handle it.

No way was he going to start stewing over this again. He'd told himself if he and Olivia could get along without fireworks, he'd take the job. He'd just seen her, they'd parted friends. Of course, he hadn't had to face Anthony fawning over her. Never mind, he could do it. End of discussion.

The Marina Inn had been built before waterfront property became so precious and it took up a lot of prime real estate. He told the valet to leave his car where it was, showing a badge to make his point, then entered the vast lobby with the three-story glass wall overlooking Puget Sound and a half dozen marinas.

He'd stayed at the place once, on his honeymoon a decade before. The hotel had thrived—the marriage had not.

He showed his badge again at the front desk and asked in which overpriced room they'd stashed a guest named Anthony Capri. The clerk was a young woman with a lilting accent and a name he couldn't pronounce. She tapped a few keys, informed him they didn't have a guest by that name. He asked if they'd had one with that name within the past two months. The woman shook her dark head and asked if he wanted to speak to the manager.

"Absolutely," he said.

The manager was a middle-aged woman with heavy black frame glasses and earrings shaped like miniature Space Needles. She was obviously fighting an allergy as she sniffed every twelve seconds. Zac knew this as he surreptitiously timed her with his watch. After much computer time, she informed him they had never had a guest named Anthony Capri, not at the Marina Inn, not even at their smaller branches, Marina Overlook and Marina Cove.

Zac went back outside and stood for a moment, taking in the fresh wind wafting off the water, the snapping flags atop masts of million-dollar yachts, the tangy, salty taste of the air. Now what?

He finally took out his cell, punched in Faith's number and left a message. She called him back a few minutes later after she'd checked with Olivia. Yep, he had the right hotel. Which must mean Anthony had lied about where he was staying.

Why would he lie about something like that? What if the hospital had tried to reach him, what if they'd called the front desk and asked for him by name?

Hadn't Faith done that very thing and assumed the hotel was the one with the problem? A would-be caller would proceed to leave a message on Anthony's cell and sooner or later, Capri would check his messages. Zac would bet a million dollars that if questioned, Capri could come up with a perfectly reasonable sounding explanation for the confusion.

He got back in the car at last. Olivia must know something else that would help him figure out what was going on. She'd been defensive when he asked her questions, reminding him of when she'd been a kid and he'd caught her in his bedroom with Faith. The two of them had dug around in his closet until they found his stash of X-rated magazines. Faith had had the grace to turn bright red and stutter. Olivia had turned the tables and chided him for looking at pictures of naked women.

The memory of her distant fierce stance still made him smile, but now was not the time for false bravado. Now was the time for candor.

Part of him said he should find someone else in the department to look for this guy, someone not fond of the man's wife.

Someone who wasn't involved.

Someone who didn't die a little inside every time he saw her.

He gritted his teeth and tossed that kind of thinking aside.

He'd do this as her friend in an unofficial way. He'd do whatever he could to give her back to the man she'd chosen.

The phone rang and he flipped it open, expecting Faith with news about Anthony. Instead he learned his snitch—the guy he'd been going to meet within a few hours—had just taken a knife in the gut down near the shipping docks. He got in the car, put the flashing light on the roof, turned on the siren and pulled into the late afternoon traffic.

The mystery of Anthony Capri would have to wait.

THE SPECIAL CARE NURSERY looked like something out of a sci-fi movie to Olivia, with machines and tubes and isolettes that resembled miniature spaceships. To her relief, on this, the second day of their lives, all four of her children were doing well.

True, they were all under UV light as a precaution for jaundice, but that was to be expected. They all also wore tiny nose prongs for oxygen and Brianna's heart rate tended to drop on occasion, so she'd acquired an additional monitor; but the consensus seemed to be her condition wasn't life-threatening and was nothing that would keep them from taking her home.

Taking them all home.

The first time Olivia had come into this ward, she'd been afraid to touch her children and had stared at them for several moments before tentatively running a finger along Juliet's tiny arm. Twenty-four hours later, she was comfortable with them, used to how petite they were, knowledgeable about how much they needed loving strokes despite the tubes and other paraphernalia.

Snuggling them against her bare skin as she took turns nursing them felt natural and healing. Faith and her mother helped feed them with bottles, doing what Anthony should have been doing if he wasn't still MIA. All three of them sang to the babies, caressed them, and talked to them. Olivia's love for her children, as well as admiration for her selfless family and her best friend, Faith, grew with every hour.

The good news was that thanks to Zac, the police had made inquiries. Anthony wasn't in any hospital or morgue in the state. The bad news was the same. If he wasn't dead or dying, then he'd decided to cut his losses and leave. And though she hadn't seen Zac since he showed up in her room, she'd spoken to him on the phone. He was in the middle of a case, he explained, and promised he'd come talk to her as soon as he could. Something in his voice warned her she better be prepared for news she didn't want to hear.

There were only a couple of possibilities, really. Either Anthony's dead body remained undiscovered or he'd taken off. As he wasn't exactly the kind to hike into the wilderness, get bitten by a snake and crawl under a bush to die, that left the other.

She caught sight of her hand and the big Asscher-cut platinum diamond engagement ring she'd just slipped back on her finger that morning. Talk about impractical for a new mother. Why had Anthony insisted on such an outrageous ring? Better question—why had she swallowed her own modest taste and agreed to it?

She couldn't think about any of that now. Instead she gazed down at Antoinette's downy head and admired her seashell ear and her velvety skin and tried to project reassuring, calm thoughts.

The doctor said they could leave in three days. Again, she tried to clear her mind but the fact was irrefutable. The day she'd longed for was quickly approaching. Very soon, she would return home to Westerly with four small but healthy babies.

And no husband.

ZAC ENTERED the hospital lobby to a crowd consisting of a couple of camera crews and a slew of reporters, one of whom he recognized from the

Westerly Herald. He found Faith standing near a wall and joined her.

"Any news about Anthony?"

"No. Any news here?"

"Nothing." She glanced forward. He followed her gaze to a long table behind which sat Olivia flanked by her mother on one side and her two youngest sisters, Megan and Tabitha, on the other.

Olivia wore a red sweater with a scooped neckline. Her throat looked like satin, her breasts larger than they'd been before, filling the sweater in such a way it was hard not to gape. She was wearing more makeup than he'd ever seen her wear—he detected Megan's liberal hand with eyeliner and lipstick. Her hair glistened under the lights and although her mother and sisters were attractive women, Olivia outshone them by a million watts.

"You look like hell," Faith said from his side.

"Thanks."

"That's the same suit you were wearing the day before yesterday."

"Tell me something I don't know."

"Did you catch the guy who knifed your guy?"

"We think his wife did it. Hard to blame her. The guy was cheating on her with two different women. It isn't my problem anymore, though."

Faith was silent for a moment and then gasped. "You took the sheriff's job in Westerly!"

"Accepted this morning."

"That's great. I bet you're glad you took Dad's advice and didn't sell your house, aren't you?"

Zac smiled. He hadn't sold his house for one reason and it had nothing to do with advice from his father. "Did I miss anything here?"

"They're just getting started. Olivia's mother has been chatting up the reporters. She gave permission for them to take a picture of the babies and Olivia is steamed about it."

The first questions concerned the births and deliveries with a heavy emphasis on the long odds against a natural occurring quadruplet conception. Olivia politely responded to the questions, but she was definitely lacking enthusiasm. Her mother, on the other hand, expanded on Olivia's terse replies. The two sisters seemed to be suffering stage fright and sat there with deer-in-headlights stares.

Inevitably, the questions moved on to inquiries about the father. Where was he? What did he think of having four children? What about his family? All dead, what a shame. When they sensed a story behind the fact that Anthony wasn't at the hospital, the questions got more pointed and Olivia just shrugged.

But not her mom. She was prepared. She spoke clearly into the microphone as she said, "Olivia's husband is unfortunately away on business."

Olivia scanned the room as her mother spoke. Her gaze landed on Zac with an almost physical jolt. He knew she was desperate for information. He had little to tell her, but her reaction upon seeing him hadn't gone unnoticed by a nearby cameraman who turned the camera on Zac. It seemed everyone in the room swiveled their heads in his direction. Zac resisted the urge to throw an arm across his face. A reporter shouted, "Is this man your husband, Mrs. Capri?"

"He's just a friend," Olivia's mother said before Olivia could respond. Juliet produced a large, professional-looking wedding picture of Anthony and Olivia. That surprised Zac as he'd heard the photographer's studio burned to the ground before the photographs were developed. Nevertheless, Juliet had managed to salvage a picture and she held it up. The cameraman zeroed in on it.

"This man is Olivia's husband, Anthony Capri, a very successful entrepreneur," Juliet said with pride. Zac didn't really think Juliet was a snob, but when her husband had died, she'd gone from being a rich woman to being poor as a church mouse. Olivia's marrying Anthony Capri must have thrilled her beyond reason.

"You've only been married a few months, isn't that true, Mrs. Capri?" one of the reporters asked.

"Yes."

"If he's so successful, why didn't he take time off for such an important event?" This came from a woman reporter on the side.

Olivia's dark eyes flashed. "I know he wanted to be here."

"Where did you say he went?"

"I didn't," she said, doubt sneaking into her voice. "He didn't have a chance to tell me."

It appeared all the reporters, who had been growing bored with another multiple baby story, smelled fresh blood. "Would you say your husband is a secretive man?"

"Absolutely not," Olivia said immediately, but her eyes betrayed her uncertainty. She squared her shoulders and added, "Anthony tells me everything. We're partners, there are no secrets between us. It's just that lately I've been out of the loop. I'm sure you understand."

Partners. Did Olivia really believe she and Anthony were partners?

He looked around the room. He could see the hunger in the reporter's eyes, the cameraman next to him zooming in closer and closer on Olivia's face. The headlines would read, *Woman Gives Birth to Quadruplets, Dad Disappears.* His heart went out to her. They had to find Anthony and nip this thing in the bud.

"What's next for you, Mrs. Capri?" someone asked.

"I just want to take my babies back to Westerly. I want to take them home."

"With your husband?"

"That goes without saying."

"That's enough," Juliet said, casting her daughter a concerned mom type glance. Amid much grumbling, the crowd began to disperse. Zac caught up with Olivia by the elevator and greeted her family, who explained they were on their way upstairs to feed and cuddle the infants. He asked Olivia to linger behind for a moment.

Faith, who had trailed him, hustled the family onto the elevator. "Catch up with us when you can," she murmured as the doors slid shut.

He put a hand under Olivia's elbow and guided her to a small sofa across the room from where the hospital maintenance crew was in the process of dismantling the table and chairs used for the interview. Their corner of the lobby was quiet.

Her mouth set in a straight line, she said, "I can't believe those reporters. They were digging for some kind of intrigue."

Zac tried to look sympathetic, but his own chore lay ahead and he dreaded it. "There's no way to sugarcoat what I have to tell you. Anthony was not staying at the Marina Inn." He hadn't told her this on the phone because it had seemed cruel to do so. Then he'd gotten waylaid by his case and finally, like the big chicken he was, he'd hoped Anthony would come to his senses and Olivia might never have to know her husband lied to her.

The time for that kind of sensibility was over as the man was still missing.

She blinked a couple of times. "What do you mean? He checked out?"

"He was never there."

"But he said he was."

Zac waited without speaking.

She blinked thick black lashes a few times, her dark eyes almost liquid. "He lied to me."

The last forty-eight hours of little sleep—and none of it in an actual bed—had made his head fuzzy, his eyelids feel grainy. Sidestepping the lying thing, he said, "I saw your mother hold up a wedding picture. If you'll get her to loan it to me I'll take it back to the hotel and find out if anyone recognizes him."

"You're saying he used a different name."

"I'm not saying anything. It's the next logical step."

She peered closely at him for a second. "You look tired, Zac."

"Nothing eight hours in the sack won't take care of. Go get the picture. I'll wait right here for you."

She nodded once and got to her feet, moving a little slowly, no doubt due to the recent operation. Her soft gray skirt swished against her long legs as she paused in front of him.

When had he first started noticing things like Olivia's breasts and shapely legs and the way her supple body curved? When had he noticed she was no longer a kid? When she came home from college to help out her mother and little sisters after her father died? He'd been in the middle of a divorce. He could barely remember anything from around that time, but at some point it had finally registered in his sorry brain that she'd changed.

And yet he'd never done a damn thing about it. The timing was always off. The chance she'd laugh in his face—well, there was that, too.

"I'll be right back but it might take a few moments," she said and he realized he'd been staring at her lips.

"I'll wait right here," he said, and watched her cross the lobby, her gait cautious but fluid. There was nothing wrong with the way her hips moved, either.

Not a damn thing.

OLIVIA CHECKED on each of her babies, leaning close to them, whispering assurances, kissing silky foreheads, promising each she would find their daddy. They indiscriminately threw their little arms wide or jerked their tiny legs up against their chests and made baby faces that charmed her down to her toes.

Olivia told Faith where she was going and while her mother was busy cooing over Brianna, swiped the lone wedding picture from the oversize handbag.

She stared at it on the way down in the elevator, bypassing her own face to concentrate on Anthony's.

The wedding had taken place in September. Anthony had been very tan, his light hair bleached lighter by months of summer sun. He looked like the sportsman he was, like a skier or a deep-sea fisherman. His white teeth glowed in contrast to his bronzed skin. With a bittersweet jab in the heart, she remembered their Key West honeymoon. He'd been attentive, charming. His smile never seemed to slip off his face. More than once she'd found herself thinking she'd married a very good actor and then reproached herself and wondered where such a thought came from.

The moment they'd returned home, she'd started throwing up. The diagnosis she was carrying multiples came next. In a daze she'd come home from the doctor's office, the sonogram clutched in her hand. She would have to tell Anthony there were four little hearts, four little lives—she would have to tell him their future had just been rewritten, things were going to change forever and ever.

He'd seemed as shocked by the news as she was. A week later, she'd begun to adjust to her new reality and a week after that, when she told Faith and her mother, she'd started looking forward to this life-altering experience.

Anthony, however, hadn't.

Slowly, as Anthony's summer tan faded with the advent of winter, so had his interest in her. He'd married a woman eager for adventure and ended up with a nauseated blimp. The fancy sports car would have to go—they would need a van of some kind. The guest suite in the house he was building acquired a new designation: nursery wing.

And now it appeared it had just been too much for him.

She found Zac exactly where she'd left him, slouched into the cushions of the sofa, arm bent, head propped on hand, legs sprawled out in front. His eyes were closed, his breathing deep. He was obviously asleep.

He wasn't tan and he didn't smile all that much. The broken nose and the scars gave his face character, enhanced his masculinity, in fact. Why hadn't he married again, had his one short marriage ruined him for love?

She'd known him since they were both kids. As her best friend's older brother, he'd ignored her, tortured her, teased her, told her to get lost, even kissed her on the lips once, long, long ago. He'd comforted her on occasion, he'd chewed her out and challenged her.

She extended a hand to shake him awake and paused, reluctant to touch him, uncertain why. She felt a nervous flutter in her stomach, her pulse rang in her ears. Where was all this coming from? Had she eaten that day? Was that it? Was she hungry?

No. Not hungry.

After a few moments he spoke without opening his eyes. "Did you get it?"

"Yes."

He held out a hand as his eyes opened. The intense blue pierced her, grounded her, chased away fanciful thoughts she had no business entertaining.

"I'm going with you," she said.

"But the babies—"

"Are with their grandma and aunties and Faith, one adult per child. They'll be fine for a while and this new mom could use an outing." She stared hard at him, daring him to refuse her. Did he understand she *had* to go, she *had* to know? Anthony Capri was her husband, the father of her children. She owed it to all of them to figure out what was going on.

He said, "Sure. No problem."

It was a cool day, making Olivia glad Faith had bought her a sweater for the press conference. It felt so good to walk on a sidewalk—she could see her own feet again!—to slide into the front seat of a car unaided. Heck, it felt good to fit in the car without pushing the seat so far back it hit the trunk. Her pregnancy had been relatively uneventful, but that still meant months of bed rest, months of being stuck indoors. She was sick of the Internet, books, television and staring out windows. She'd missed the smell of fresh air, the feel of the wind ruffling her hair as she ran, even the cool dampness of the fog swirling overhead.

She offered to drive but Zac refused, claiming his catnap had refreshed him. He seemed revitalized, his driving as sharp and crisp as ever even if he drove slower than she would have.

Olivia couldn't keep from counting the motels and hotels they passed. Nineteen of them between the hospital and the Marina Inn. Anthony had bypassed nineteen opportunities to be closer to her.

Except apparently he hadn't stayed at the Marina Inn after all.

"How's it feel to be free?" Zac asked.

She looked over at his familiar profile, so glad they were friends again. "Like heaven."

"How much longer do you have to stay at the hospital?"

"Technically, I'm already rooming with Faith at a place across the street, but in reality, I'm living more or less in the nursery. My mom and sisters are going back to Westerly tomorrow."

"Have all the babies reached four pounds yet?"

"Not all of them. The doctors want them to stay another few days, but I don't know. We have an excellent hospital in Westerly, as you know. My sister in California is on her way, too."

"Sandy?"

"Yep. The doctor seemed impressed I'd have a real live nurse in residence for two weeks. I think he can be persuaded to let the babies leave a little early. I hope so. I want to go home."

He gestured at the wedding photo Olivia held on her lap. "I thought the photo place burned down while you were on your honeymoon?"

"Right before we left. Mom took this picture herself without telling us and had it blown up. Anthony didn't want a bunch of amateurish photographs floating around. However, you know Mom. She wanted one of her own so she snapped this without him knowing it."

She gazed down at the photo again. Her own face

wreathed in smiles, Anthony's tall well-built shape towering over her. He was looking to the right of the camera, holding a champagne flute. Sunlight glinted off the gold and diamonds of the Super Bowl ring he always wore, claiming it was impossible to get off his finger as he'd gained weight since first putting it on.

She'd been blown away by the intensity of their whirlwind romance and had allowed herself to be swept into the exciting world he proposed. It was as though he'd known exactly what she wanted—and what her life lacked—and offered it on a silver platter. She'd convinced herself his love was real and that hers was real, too. She'd married him nine weeks after they met.

Nine weeks!

She dug in her handbag for her house keys. On the ring with the keys was a small pocket knife that also housed a pair of scissors. With a few quick stokes, she cut the photo in half, putting the half with her image and the knife back in her purse.

Zac watched her do this without saying a thing.

They pulled into the hotel parking lot. Olivia struggled a bit getting out of the low-slung car, glad when Zac lent a hand.

Using his badge to grease the way around the long line of guests waiting to check in, Zac showed the wedding photo to the staff. "Have any of you seen this man before?"

Almost everyone at the counter recognized Anthony. "That's Mr. Gray," a woman with beautiful slanted eyes said. "Paul Gray."

"He's a NASCAR driver," a kid in a bowtie said.

"And a deep-sea diver," another added. "And a Super Bowl star."

"He tipped like there was no tomorrow."

"'Tipped' as in past tense?" Zac said.

"Well, yeah. He checked out yesterday."

Yesterday! Two days after the babies' births? Olivia didn't know what she'd expected to hear, but this wasn't it. And since when had Anthony driven NASCAR? Her stomach did a backflip and she leaned against the marble counter for support.

Zac said, "Did he say where he was going?"

"Home," the first young man said without hesitation. "He said his wife was having a baby and he had to get home."

"Did he say where home was?"

"Uh, I don't think so."

"Local," the woman said. "He seemed very well-acquainted with Seattle."

"He went out every night he was here. Really nice guy. Really generous."

"Did he seem distracted or upset when he checked out?"

They all looked at each other and shook their heads.

"Think carefully," Zac said after a moment. "Was he alone when he checked out?"

"There were people in the lobby," one girl said.

"No there weren't. It was mid-morning and all the business people had left," the boy insisted.

"No, there was a kind of jumpy guy over by the potted palms and a woman and two teenagers by the elevators."

The boy shrugged. "He had the valet bring his car around," he volunteered.

"What kind of car, do you remember? A van?" This from Olivia.

"No, a sleek white coupe," the girl said. "Joey, didn't you take a picture of him with Alyssa and Tommy?"

"Sure," one of the boys said, and rummaged in a pocket. Out came the ubiquitous cell phone.

Olivia's gaze fastened on Anthony, smiling as usual. Green numerals flashing on the screen identified the date as the day before. It had been taken in front of the Inn and in the background she could make out what appeared to be her white car.

She suddenly couldn't bear to stand there a second longer. She turned on her heels, and heedless of the spasm of pain the jerky movement caused, kept on going toward the front door, quaking inside.

She made it outside before she could go no further. Bending at the waist, she clasped her thighs. Tears dripped onto the pavement by her feet. A small knot of tourists looked away as though embarrassed for her.

She couldn't stop the tears. She could barely catch a breath. *So, this is what it's like when your life falls apart...*

She saw Zac's shoes before she heard his voice. He put a warm hand on her back and she straightened up, leaning against him as he ushered her out of the traffic pattern.

"Are you all right?"

She said, "No," but a new thought had just struck her.

"Let me take you back to the hospital," Zac murmured.

"I want to go to Westerly."

"But—"

"They said he went home."

"Olivia, please—"

"Maybe, maybe he took my car home to get the van to come back for me and the babies. Maybe there's some kind of explanation. I have to know. I have to go look. Either drive me there or I'll drive myself."

"You're in no shape—"

She started walking toward his car, though she couldn't feel her feet hit the pavement and could barely see through the tears and the burn of dissolving mascara.

"Olivia—"

She paused, turning to look back at him.

"Wait up," he said.

Chapter Three

Zac navigated Seattle's busy streets as Olivia left a message for Faith to return her call. He drove as she waited anxiously, leaning forward against her seat belt.

The phone finally rang as they crossed the bridge and merged onto the highway leading southwest. Olivia answered immediately, her voice strained. Her first questions concerned her babies, then she told Faith where they were going, promising to be back at the hospital in four hours. As it took most of an hour to get to Westerly and the same to get back, that left them little time to look around town. He wasn't sure what she expected to accomplish, but he wasn't about to argue with her.

Thanks to light traffic, they made good time, but the fog came with them, trailing for a while, then encompassing the vehicle and the cities through which they passed. By the time they left the highway, the world was gray.

Westerly was one of those towns that had grown up a hundred years earlier around a lumber mill situated on Puget Sound. The mill was long gone and thus the town had had to reinvent itself, evolving at last into something of an artist community, which had the added benefit of attracting tourists. As a result, downtown was old but lively, heavy on flower boxes, summer festivals, murals and galleries. Neighborhoods were split between old Victorians close in and new hillside developments. The citizenry was equally split between those who could trace their roots back three generations and those who had moved there within the past ten years.

"Where do you want to check first?" Zac asked as they eased past the Welcome to Westerly sign that now sported an additional banner, barely visible through the fog: Westerly Welcomes Home Its Four Newest Citizens, the Capri Quadruplets! Congratulations, Anthony and Olivia!"

"Notice how they put his name first?" Olivia said. He glanced at her, relieved the tears were gone. She met his gaze and added, "He wouldn't come back here if his intent was to run away, would he?"

"I don't think so." Zac thought this would be the last place on earth Anthony would consider a retreat. It was his wife's hometown, he was almost a celebrity here himself.

Man, if Capri had skipped, there was going to be

hell to pay in more ways than the humiliating mess Olivia would have to face. The man had taken well over a million dollars from the Robinson brothers and neither of them would accept that kind of loss with anything resembling grace. They wouldn't see their own greed. Would they try to sue Olivia? In a New York minute. Not every citizen of Westerly was compassionate.

Nope, if Anthony had reneged on loans at the bank or absconded with investment dollars it was going to be a class-A disaster.

"Let's go to my house," she said, slinking down in the seat. She'd been wiping at her makeup as they drove and now her dark eyes looked even darker in her pale face. It was obvious she didn't want this to be her big homecoming. He didn't want it to be his, either. He had a few more days to report for work, days he should spend moving his stuff between Seattle and Westerly, but first things first. He left the main street quickly, taking an obscure route. "Which house? The one you guys are building?"

"No, take me to the one I've lived in for the past six years, the rental on Queen Street. I'm sure Anthony's emptied the house by now, but maybe he went there for some reason and it's closer."

"Maybe," Zac said. Maybe he went there to pack up the rest of his stuff and hightail it on out of town.

"It's where we lived until we left Westerly," she continued, her voice scratchy. "It's a place to start."

In other words, Zac thought as he turned down Queen Street less than five minutes later, it was home to Olivia. In her heart of hearts, she must think it was home to Capri, as well. Zac doubted it.

Olivia's house was on the far corner. As he drove down the long driveway, she opened her handbag and withdrew the garage opener. She punched it once and the door slid open to reveal a very new white luxury car parked in the garage.

"He must be here," she said.

Zac was surprised, to say the least. And confused. What was this guy up to? "Why was he driving this? I thought he had a red sports car."

"That was a lease. We agreed we'd buy a van for the babies and he could use my car because it was bought and paid for. He wanted to wait a few months for the new models to come out before he got himself something else." She paused a second and added, "He told me a couple of weeks ago that he bought the van. Maybe it's parked at the new house."

"Do you want me to wait—"

"No," she said. "I don't trust myself alone with him."

They got out of the car and walked toward the sheltered back door that led directly into the kitchen.

OLIVIA STEELED HERSELF.

The last time she'd been in this house, she'd been leaving for her extended hospital stay as the doctors told her the contractions she'd experienced could mean trouble and she needed to get off and stay off her feet. That meant an extended trip to Seattle's new neonatal care unit.

She remembered Anthony walking ahead of her as she descended the stairs, talking all the time about how she'd never have to live in this old dump again, that by the time the babies came, the new house on the point would be ready for occupancy.

She remembered being pleased he was so excited about making their lives more comfortable, but she'd also been—she could admit it now—a little hurt. This place might be a rental, but she loved its old Victorian styling, the high ceilings, the tall windows, the gingerbread trim and the turret room she used as an office.

She braced herself to have it out with him—if he was still here. He had some explaining to do.

Zac took her key and opened the door, stopping so abruptly after stepping inside that she bumped into him. "Oh, no."

She looked past him and for the second time that day, felt herself sway on her feet.

He reached back. "You okay?"

Grateful for the support of his arm, she could

manage nothing more than a deep breath and a slight nod. For a few moments they stood in silence gazing at the destruction before them.

Every cupboard door stood ajar, the contents thrown on the counters and floor. Every drawer torn from the counters and overturned. Layers of crushed dry goods covered broken dishes and silverware. The open refrigerator poured cold air into the room, though what little food remained inside had begun to smell. The freezer, equally gutted, sent forth rivulets of water and melted ice cream that snaked across the old uneven floor, mingling with every-thing else.

Olivia, speechless, hugged herself as a wave of nausea rolled through her stomach.

"We need to call the sheriff's department," Zac said.

"Where's Anthony? I have to look. I won't touch anything."

They carefully negotiated the quagmire of the kitchen floor, moving into the living room. It, too, had been torn asunder, books thrown from shelves, upholstery split and gutted, rugs slashed and pulled up. It didn't look to Olivia as though Anthony had removed one item from this place. How had he expected they were going to get by with four babies and no furniture in the new house?

"Anthony?" she called. The house was silent except for the noise from the refrigerator.

"It looks as though someone was looking mighty hard for something," Zac said.

"But what?" she whispered. Another thought hit. "My office, all my clients' records…"

"I'll go look," he said and climbed the stairs to the turret room, returning a few minutes later, shaking his head. "It's the same. There's a blizzard of paper everywhere, though the computer and printer look undamaged."

"Was the safe untouched?"

"Yes."

"That's where I keep most of the important records anyway. Not that there are many left. I had to take a break from bookkeeping when I learned about the quads."

She stumbled on a broken lamp as she moved and he grasped her arms. "Steady."

"I want to see the bedrooms," she said. "Especially the one we used." It was where she kept keepsakes. Most of Anthony's stuff had been in boxes in the basement though it might be at the new house by now. She took a few steps, trying to prepare herself for what she'd find.

The door opened onto a room that looked much as it had when she left it, down to her old robe hanging on a hook behind the door. There were broken and misplaced things in here in here, too, but very little as though the search had only gotten started when something or someone interrupted it. Tears rolled down her cheeks and whether they were tears of loss, anger or relief that at least a few of her things had remained unscathed, she didn't know.

There on the vanity was the ditty box her sea faring father had left her as his oldest daughter, filled with mementos from his youth. Next to it, a shallow box holding Anthony's spare watch and cufflinks though some of the items had been scattered across the top. A couple of the drawers were open, some of the clothes dumped on the floor, but not bad. On top of the armoire, next to a plaster bell Anthony's mother had made, were six porcelain dolls she'd bequeathed him. No wait, there were just five now, one was on the floor in a dozen pieces.

She twirled around suddenly, looking for her mother's old jewelry box and found it where it was supposed to be except the lid was open. She crossed to peer inside. It looked the same as always. The hope chest, filled with linens hand embroidered by her grandmother, remained locked. Peeking through the closet door, Anthony's clothes, his jackets, slacks, shoes…

"Whoever it was didn't get far in here," Zac said.

"They must have been interrupted." Olivia was confused. Why had Anthony moved nothing out of this house, not even his personal items or hers? They'd discussed all this several times. She wanted to decorate the new house herself, but that wouldn't be practical at first so Anthony would move things over, then after she got home and somehow found a little time, she'd start furnishing the much larger house.

If he hadn't moved anything did that mean the new house wasn't finished? Or did it mean something worse?

"Olivia? You've gone all quiet on me."

"What if Anthony came back here to get our things and walked in on a burglary?"

"Then where is he?"

She looked around frantically. "I don't know. Maybe they kidnapped him."

Guilt seeped through her pores, covering her body in a thin layer of sweat. She'd been angry with Anthony for not appearing when he said he would and now she was sure he had been waylaid by evil thugs. She'd misjudged him. She'd been selfish and so caught up in herself—

"Why?" Zac said.

"Why? Why what?"

"If he walked in on them and they bopped him on the head, why didn't they finish the job and take the jewelry or the computer upstairs or the new television? Why did they leave all the valuable stuff?"

"Because they were afraid someone would come looking for him?"

"Okay, then where is he now? Why didn't he alert anyone?"

"I don't know. Maybe someone kidnapped him…"

"I'll take the basement, you look in the other two bedrooms. Holler if you need me."

THE BASEMENT APPEARED untouched though it had acquired new furniture since Zac had seen it last. He checked out every closet, bypassing the untouched stack of cardboard boxes marked "Private, Keep Out," in the corner. Nothing. No one.

It annoyed the hell out of him that Olivia was blaming herself for doubting her husband. The man had done nothing but lie to her and yet she was still trying to give him a break. She'd apparently forgotten he'd been half an hour away the day after their children came into the world. What kind of excuse could pardon that behavior?

And what had happened in this house? Why had it been searched, and that it had was obvious to him. So where was the guy, why hadn't he reported this intrusion? The police had made a thorough check of every unidentified male victim in the last three days and none of them matched Anthony's description.

A muffled scream sounded from above. Taking the stairs two at a time, Zac reached the main floor and jumped over an overturned chair, sliding as he landed on a pile of books. His reaction had come straight from his gut, not professional at all, and he slowed down, reaching under his jacket for his gun.

"In here," Olivia called from the hallway, her voice shaky. She stepped out of the last room, the one before the bathroom. Her face was as white as the plaster wall she gripped. "Come look."

He joined her quickly and immediately saw what had alarmed her. The room had been ransacked like the others, but unlike the others there were blood spatters against the wall and desk front.

"Stand right here while I check every closet. Don't move."

Gun drawn, he made a thorough check of the house. Anthony wasn't in it, nor was he in the car in the garage or the garage either, for that matter. Zac went back for Olivia, who was standing with her back against the wall, eyes closed.

"We're calling the sheriff's department," he said.

Her eyes flew open. "I can't just wait—"

"We'll sit in my car. Come on."

They carefully threaded their way through the house, trying to retrace their steps and not disturb anything more than they already had. As they left the house she said, "Let me have your keys."

"Why?"

"Because I'm driving."

"Driving where? We're staying right here—"

"Give me your keys. Please, Zac."

He took his keys from his pocket and handed them over.

"I'll come back, I promise."

"I'll go with you."

"No, you don't have to—"

"Olivia, let's just do it." Whatever *it* was.

Once in the car, she opened the garage door again and sped backward down the narrow driveway, hitting the street and turning east on Queen.

"The sheriff's department is the other way," he said as he took out his cell phone.

"Make your call, do what you need to do."

"Where are we going, Olivia?"

"I'm doing what I need to do."

He wasn't sure what that meant, but Westerly was, after all, a small town and it soon became obvious what her intentions were. He called the sheriff's office, identifying himself to Terry, who always manned the phone on weekends. "I want a crime scene team sent pronto to Olivia Hart's house, 333 Queen Street."

"Capri," Olivia said tersely.

"Oh, yeah. Sorry. Olivia and Anthony Capri. Be advised there was a break-in, blood in the second bedroom. I'll check in again in awhile. Call in Hoopes and Dilly." He hung up before Terry could ask him what he was doing acting like sheriff, assigning duty and all the rest before he was actually sheriff or why he wasn't sticking around at the scene to meet the cops at the house. He didn't have answers to those questions.

"You're going to the new house," he said as Olivia took a corner too fast and the rear end of the car swerved toward the verge. "Slow down," he added. "You've always driven too fast."

"I'm a little anxious," she said without taking her eyes from the road.

"You also have four kids. They need you. Slow down."

She slowed but it really had little to do with him and more to do with turning off the main highway onto a dirt road. It meandered through the trees for half a mile before stopping in a clearing.

Perched on the edge of the point with what he assumed would be close to a one-hundred-and-eighty-degree view of Puget Sound when the fog cleared, stood a huge house made of wood and glass, surrounded with covered tiered decks disappearing into the gloom.

The land itself had yet to be groomed and looked like a construction site before the crew cleans up after itself. Remnants of roofing material, siding and concrete blocks littered the ground that would someday be sweeping lawns.

"This is some mansion," Zac said, and maybe for the first time, the scope of Anthony Capri's wealth hit him full-on. The house looked more like a resort. It had to be at least six or seven thousand square feet.

"Out in the middle of nowhere," Olivia said as she turned off the engine. "Anthony says there's a natural inlet right around the point. Not that you can see it with this fog."

"I just can't get over how gigantic it is."

"He'd started on it well before we got together," she said. "Well, at least it doesn't look as though he lied to me about the house being finished. I mean the yard is a mess but we can…" her voice trailed off as though she didn't know how to end that sentence. Given the events of the past few days, Zac couldn't blame her.

She slid out of the car, digging in her bag for her keys again. "I'm surprised there's no security system," he said as they walked up broad wooden stairs.

"Anthony said there was some kind of factory delay. It's supposed to be installed next week."

She opened the door, walked inside and he followed. They both stopped almost at once.

It was like walking into a wooden beast, the inside simply a skeleton supporting the outside layer of siding and roof. Standing in what would someday be the spacious front room, they could see through the gaps between the hundreds of vertical two-by-fours to the shimmer of glass in the back.

"He lied to me," she said. "Again."

"He told you it was ready for occupancy?"

"Yes."

Zac gestured toward a far corner. "I think I see something dense back that way."

"That's the nursery wing," she mumbled. He took her arm as they passed a massive stone fireplace and walked through the structure, treating the framing like real walls. Zac could see no sign of plumbing or electricity. The place was a long way from finished and he thought back to the only other home Olivia had—the one that had been torn apart and spattered with blood.

They turned a corner into a series of rooms that opened off a central area. "This will be the play area," she said softly. "The rooms open off of it. The master suite is through there to the south."

Windows showcased only the fog outside, but she seemed driven to walk toward the feeble light. Meanwhile, Zac made his way toward a pile of unopened boxes fresh from the shipper. They formed the solid mass he'd seen from the front and all but blocked the double single-pane glass French doors behind them. He could make out a few of the labels. Cribs, changing tables, car seats, bassinets, even clothing and diapers and four rocking chairs.

She came to stand beside him. "That's the stuff I ordered off the Internet while I was stuck in the hospital. I had it shipped directly here." She ran a hand over one of the boxes and added, "Anthony told me last week that he'd assembled the bassinets. Surprise, he lied."

She turned away, burying her face in her hands. Zac stood there watching her shoulders shake and didn't know what to say or do. He longed to comfort her but he didn't trust himself.

How long had he loved her like this?

Loved her to the point it was torture being around her?

She turned slowly, dropping her hands, and their eyes met. Hers were like dark holes in the universe, sucking him in, her pain and need more than he could bear. He told himself to act like the friend he was supposed to be and opened his arms. She slowly stepped into his embrace and rested her head against his shoulder. He closed his eyes, way too aware of the silky ambrosia of her hair against his cheek, her breasts pressed against his chest, her warmth and softness. He'd touched her a thousand times over the years but never once like this and the fact it was all one-sided, the fact her tears were on another's man's behalf made him ashamed of his feelings.

"I'm not a crier," she snuffled after a few moments, gazing up at him.

"You could have fooled me," he said with a dismal attempt at humor. He ran a couple of fingers across her tear-stained cheek as they looked into each other's eyes. The moment seemed to linger, dragging its feet like a lover reluctant to depart. "It's not a crime to break down," he added.

She heaved a sigh and stepped away. "Anthony is in some kind of trouble, isn't he?"

"It appears so," Zac said, watching as she dug in her handbag for tissues. The little package was empty. He took a clean folded handkerchief from his pocket and handed it to her.

"I know I should be worried about him, but frankly, I'm more worried about my babies and what all this means to them."

"I don't blame you. Just remember you're not alone."

When she raised her eyebrows, he mumbled, "The whole town will stand behind you, Olivia. And you know you can depend on Faith."

"I know," she said softly.

"The search for Anthony will take on a new dimension now there's the potential of a crime being committed."

"To him or by him?"

"I don't know, Olivia."

"I just don't understand why he did all this," she whispered, wiping her eyes. "I don't understand why he pursued me and married me and then why he stuck around until the babies were born but never bothered to come see them. Did he steal money, is that it, Zac? Or did he do something worse?"

"I don't know that either, honey," he said. "We'll find out."

She nodded and stood there and then suddenly said, "Where are all my shower gifts?"

"What shower gifts?"

"Faith gave me a baby shower. Everyone came. Everyone brought me wonderful things. What did Anthony do with it all? Some of it was handmade or antique…Did you see baby things in the basement on Queen Street?"

"No. Nothing down there but a giant pool table and a big flat screen TV. Oh, and a pile of boxes marked Private."

"Anthony's stuff. Maybe he moved the shower things over here for some reason."

Zac looked through the forest of framing and said, "And hid them—where?"

"Maybe the garage. Maybe they poured the cement floor."

Considering the unfinished state of the house, Zac thought that very unlikely, but he followed along as she led the way through one vast unfinished room after the other. He couldn't imagine why she was worrying about more baby stuff unless it seemed like something she could handle while everything else spun out of her control.

They walked through what would someday be a huge dining room and kitchen, through a laundry area, and down through a causeway. Olivia opened up a door into what appeared to be a five- or six-stall garage. Empty. All that was there was a deep layer of sand, a few scattered tools and an old blue yard tarp. The place smelled earthy.

"What's under the tarp?"

"It better not be the things from the shower," she said with an ominous sound to her voice. She'd already covered half the distance, making her way slowly through the sand. Her stamina, given she was still recovering from an operation, staggered him. It helped, he supposed, to be so preoccupied.

"It wouldn't make sense to stick them out here," she added as she tugged on a corner of the tarp.

There was nothing beneath it.

"Well at least—" she began and then something apparently caught her eye and she knelt. "It's Anthony's Super Bowl ring," she said, kneeling gingerly to pick it up. She glanced at Zac and added, "It's not like him to leave it laying—"

And in that instant, Zac's sorry excuse for a brain kicked into gear. Dark stains on the sand, parallel tracks as though something heavy had been dragged across it, a shovel off to the side…

"Olivia, stop!" he yelled as he sprang forward, but by then, she'd brushed the sand away and was yanking hard, as though meeting resistance. Along with the ring, she pulled up a man's chalky hand. Sand rolled off the attached sleeve…

She threw her hands up and the arm thudded against the sand. A deep moan erupted from her throat as she stumbled backward, bumping into Zac. She turned into his chest and buried her face, her body shaking.

Judging from the flashy ring and the snug way it fit the dead man's finger, Anthony Capri was no longer missing.

Chapter Four

"Hell of a way to start your job as sheriff," Detective Roger Dilly said.

Dilly was a slight man with quick dark eyes. Wearing a perfectly tailored tan Westerly Sheriff Department uniform, gleaming black shoes and a sidearm on his hip, he always reminded Zac of fictional Deputy Barney Fife.

Zac rubbed bloodshot eyes and nodded, watching the preliminary examination of the body by Doc Wheeler. Even Zac could see what had killed Capri: multiple shots in the back. "Technically, I'm not sheriff until day after tomorrow," he said. "In fact, you're in charge right now, aren't you?"

Dilly lifted an eyebrow. "I was but I'm not now."

"I'm not going to come in here early and—"

"I've never conducted a murder investigation," Dilly said. "The council will swear you in tomorrow. It's all yours. I'll do whatever you need, though, you know that."

Zac nodded once. Doc Wheeler stood up from where he'd been crouching. "I guess you can see what killed him," he said.

"Yeah. Any way to tell when?"

"From the degree of rigor, I'd say less than twenty-four hours ago."

The hotel staff had said he checked out the morning before. As it was going on 9:00 p.m. now, that meant Capri drove back to Westerly and got himself killed sometime between noon and nine of the day before. It also meant the case was a day old already. Doc picked up his satchel. "I'll do an autopsy in the morning, but right now it looks like there were a few pre-mortem abrasions on his face. His ring finger on the right hand is bruised—my guess is someone tried to get that ring off his finger. I bagged his hands because the knuckles are raw as though he landed a punch or two. I'll know more tomorrow."

"Thanks, Doc."

Doc tipped his hat, a baseball cap he'd worn for at least twenty years, and ambled off after the body being carried away on a gurney.

Zac turned to Dilly. "I've been away for several months. Tell me what you know about Capri's movements lately."

"Not much. He wasn't in Westerly often, we all thought he was up at the hospital with Olivia.

Course, I don't think finding the killer is going to be hard."

"And why is that?"

"I don't think we're going to have to look too much further than one of the Robinson brothers. Or maybe both. Grant's been telling anyone who would listen what a con man Capri was and that he and Hugh planned to do something about it. What about you? You think Capri was a con man?"

"Yeah," Zac said. "I do."

"Hmm. Last summer I was kicking myself because I didn't have any money to invest with the guy. Guess I lucked out."

"I don't know for sure," Zac said.

"I caught the press conference on the news tonight. Olivia looked good, but they made Capri sound like he was on the lam or something."

Zac shrugged. He'd forgotten all about the press conference. "Local station?"

"No, the mystery behind the no-show father of quadruplets made it bigger than local. The networks got hold of it, too. They're going to have a heyday when they get wind the missing father was killed the day after his babies were born and not fifty miles away."

Zac clenched jaw muscles. That meant the national news would replay Olivia's assertion that she and her husband were partners and had no secrets from each other. Seeing as Anthony had been murdered, that wasn't a good place to be for Olivia. "Then I guess we better get this solved," Zac said. "Olivia and her family don't need the distractions of the press."

"I sent a couple of the new guys out to ask the neighbors if they heard gunfire last night. Must have been a hell of a racket."

Zac looked out the garage door at the tall trees rising above the thinning fog. The wind had kicked up and was blowing the murk back out over the water revealing a dock attached to the house by a ramp. "It's pretty remote out here. The closest neighbor must be a half mile away."

"Maybe someone heard or saw something."

"How's Olivia taking it?"

"She seems numb," Zac said. He'd had a deputy drive her into the station so she could avoid all this. "I'm going to go pick her up and take her back to Seattle, then I'll hightail it back here."

"I can get one of the guys to drive her—"

"No, that's okay, I want to ask her a couple of questions."

"Listen, no offense, but you look beat. Catch some sleep before you drive back here, okay? We'll process this place and Olivia's house tonight. Tomorrow we'll have more information."

Zac nodded. "That'll give me a chance to go over to the Marina Inn and take a look at their security tape, make sure Anthony Capri was alone when he checked out. One of the staff said something about a guy lurking by a palm. I'll see if a camera caught a good shot of him."

Dilly cleared his throat before adding, "Capri took the bullets in his back. In my mind that looks as if he was trying to run away. Do you think his shooting was connected to the break-in at Olivia's place?"

"I think it must be. How else did Capri get out here? The car he was driving is parked in Olivia's garage. There's no vehicle here. If it was the Robinson boys, why did they tear up Olivia's house?"

"Looking for their money?"

"They think Capri hid a million dollars or more in a little old house? We need to get a bank audit on that guy, too, by the way."

"Yeah, well, if it wasn't Robinson, then it was someone else and what happens if they didn't find what they were looking for?"

"I guess they keep looking."

"Maybe they just look as far as the widow."

"I thought of that," Zac said. "That's exactly why I'm sticking close to her."

"ANTHONY IS DEAD," Olivia said into the dark car, trying out the words, taking them for a test spin.

They sounded hollow and forlorn and in some weird way, just impossible. She wanted to ask Zac to step on the gas, but she'd already asked him two or three times and reasonably, she knew they were going as fast as was safe. The need burning in her gut to get back to her babies wouldn't go away though and she tucked her hands under her thighs to keep them still.

Zac said, "I promise you, Olivia, we will find out who did this to him. You will get justice."

"The man at the station said he thought one of the Robinson brothers did it," she said softly. "He thinks Grant. I can't believe he or Hugh would do something like that to Anthony."

"Wait a second. One of the deputies speculated about this case to you?"

"No, not one of the deputies, the guy on the janitor service. I think it was the oldest Casey boy. I was lying down in Dilly's office and he came in to mop the floor and we got to talking."

"The kid was just flapping his lips. Forget about it."

She put her head against the headrest and tried to figure out what she felt deep inside about Anthony's death. The answer terrified her. Nothing. She felt nothing. She wasn't even sure who was dead because in the past three days, she'd stopped knowing who Anthony Capri really was.

Three days? Try three months. Be truthful, he's been drifting away for a long time and you knew it…

The hospital, ablaze with lights, loomed at the end of the street. Olivia scanned the side of the building, counting windows up five flights. Inside those walls were her children. Jillian, Brianna, Juliet and Antoinette. Antoinette, named after her father.

"He never even saw them," she said, bewildered by it still. "He could have but he chose not to."

"Maybe he couldn't. Maybe he thought it would be dangerous to lead anyone to you or the babies."

She looked out the window. Maybe…

"I'm sorry, Olivia, but I have to ask you a couple of questions."

"It's okay," she said, keeping her eyes on the lights ahead.

"Can you think of anyone who hated your husband, who threatened him or wanted him dead?"

"Besides the Robinson brothers? I never even heard either one of them say anything terrible about Anthony. The bad feelings must have started after I left Westerly."

"How about anyone else? Other business associates, for instance. Friends?"

"No one," she said quickly. It was the truth. She'd married Anthony in September and almost immediately left for an eight-week honeymoon in the Florida Keys. Anthony had talked to everyone they met and everyone seemed to like him. He'd made all sorts of friends at the resort. Had any of them looked or acted suspicious? No.

Then they'd come home and she'd immediately felt crummy. During those weeks, Anthony had been busy doing business in Westerly and Seattle, staying out late entertaining people—she'd been too sick to her stomach to go with him. Then she had to take it easy and her mother and sister started helping during the week, Faith on weekends and it seemed she and Anthony never had a moment alone. The hospital came next with enforced bed rest and ever diminishing visits from her husband.

"The truth is," she said bleakly, "I didn't know him very well. There wasn't time."

"The past few months do seem to have sped by," Zac said, entering the parking garage.

Glancing over at Zac, she said, "I keep thinking about that reporter. Was that just today?"

"Yesterday," Zac said, pulling into a spot in the nearly empty structure. He switched off the engine. "It's after midnight."

"Well, I keep thinking about that question, was Anthony a secretive man? The answer is yes, he was secretive, at least with me. I didn't notice it so much because he wasn't quiet, he joked and laughed and chatted so much I just never noticed he didn't really say anything important. Why didn't I notice that, Zac?"

"Olivia—"

"Because maybe if I'd asked questions or not been so absorbed in my pregnancy I would have been there for him and maybe this wouldn't have happened—"

"Don't do this to yourself," he said. He got out and walked around the trunk, opening her door, waiting as she slipped out of her seat. She was tired and she hurt both inside and outside, dull far away pain that throbbed through her body and soul. He put his hands on her shoulders and stared down at her. "I don't know what Anthony got himself into, but I do know it wasn't your fault."

Tears burned the back of her nose. She would have welcomed their release, but they didn't fall. His hands slid down her arms and he gripped her hands firmly, keeping one encased in his as they walked across the causeway and rode the elevator up to the nursery. Before she entered she pulled him back. "Zac, promise me you'll never tell my girls their father didn't come see them. I don't want them to know."

"Whatever you say."

She nodded once. A few moments later, she walked into the nursery. Faith was just putting Brianna back in her isolette. Still holding a tiny baby bottle, she closed the distance between them as Olivia's mother looked up from dozing in a rocking chair. As Faith folded Olivia in a hug, her mother joined them, putting her arms around both younger women, all three of them touching foreheads.

Olivia allowed herself a few moments of comforting and then, one by one, she visited Anthony's daughters, picking them up, nuzzling them close, inhaling their innocence as she whispered the bad news into soft little ears.

Her daughters, now. Just hers.

As somehow she'd known they would be from the day they were born.

"THREE BULLETS IN THE BACK."

Zac put the folder he was reading on top of the other ten folders he had yet to peruse and met Dilly's gaze. "What kind of weapon?"

"A .38. I sent the bullets Doc dug out of the vic along with the rest of the stuff to the lab in Seattle. But the bullets aren't what killed him. Doc says the first one severed his spine, but he was still alive when he was buried. He suffocated."

"Oh, man, that's terrible."

"Doc says that's why his hand was so close to the surface. We found a lot of blood out near the trees and a blood trail leading back to the garage. I got the boys out there combing the area. We also found a few tire imprints and one of a shoe about the same size as Capri's but with a different imprint."

"What about the blood in Olivia's house?"

"Doc Wheeler says it came from two individuals. One matches Capri's blood type."

"How about his hands. Did the doc say anything about skin caught under the fingernails or those abrasions he noticed last night?"

"Some skin under the right hand fingernails, under the sand. He still thinks Capri was in a fight before he died."

"Which could explain the blood spatter at Olivia's house. Capri must have walked in on an intruder, though why he proceeded to get in the car with the guy and take a ride out to that remote, empty house is anyone's guess. I reviewed the security tapes at the hotel. They didn't show anything useful. Listen, we need to finish up over at Olivia's place today. She's bringing the babies home in the next day or two. I need time to get someone in there to clean it up."

"Consider it done," Dilly said.

OLIVIA'S EYES WATERED as Zac drove down Main Street. Every single person in town seemed to have shown up, despite the drizzle, despite the unseasonably cold day. There was also a Metro News van and a slew of unfamiliar faces among the crowd.

Going from anonymity to newsworthy inside a few days took a little getting used to.

She was sitting in the backseat between Brianna and Antoinette. Faith sat in the seat behind her, sandwiched between Jillian and Juliet. Zac drove, Olivia's sister, Sandy, seated beside him on the long bench seat. Sandy, who had recently stopped smoking, chewed gum incessantly. Next to the window, Olivia's mother waved her hand in a pretty back-and-forth motion like someone in a homecoming parade.

Which, considering the fact this was indeed a homecoming, wasn't that unsuitable.

Back at the hospital, Zac had asked her which house she wanted to return to. She'd said, "mine," very firmly. She never wanted to see the house out on the point again, and the thought of crowding herself and four babies and all their paraphernalia into her mother's house in which her two younger sisters still resided, had seemed terrible. Zac had offered his place, but she'd declined. She just wanted to go home.

The nursing staff at the hospital had prepared her. With Faith and Sandy's help, she knew she could take care of the girls properly, despite the monitors and the oxygen and all the rest that went with very small babies. Faith had reminded her she would be around as needed and even Zac had fed a baby that morning before they departed, holding Jillian and giving her a bottle while never taking his eyes off her face. Olivia had been fascinated by the size of his hands cradling the tiny infant, and the juxtaposition of his raw maleness next to Jillian's pink-and-white fragility.

And now they were home. She looked down at Brianna's slumbering face, at her crumpled little lips and her round, soft cheeks, and felt a surge of emotion. Was Zac right? Had Anthony stayed away in an attempt to protect her and his babies?

She'd like to believe it and who knew, maybe that's the spin she would put on the story someday as the girls grew up, but for now, Olivia couldn't quite buy it. She knew from Zac they'd found Anthony's cell phone in his pocket. He'd made a couple of calls the day she gave birth—none of them to Olivia. He'd also erased several messages from her, Faith, Olivia's mom and the hospital.

And now he was dead; any chance he would have had to reinvent himself as a father was over. Someone had shot him and buried him alive.

She glanced at Antoinette, who was staring at her with drowsy slate eyes. How could such evil exist in the same world with such purity?

"We're here," Zac announced from the front seat.

Olivia looked up. More tears gathered in her eyes as she took in the sight of her neighbors lining her driveway. She steeled herself for all the commotion that was sure to come, knowing it originated from good hearts and concern, but also knowing it would be taxing. She was finding that fatigue was a new mom's middle name.

AN HOUR LATER, Olivia stood in her living room and looked around, absolutely amazed at the transformation of her house.

The last time she'd seen it the place had been a wreck, but that wasn't the case anymore. Olivia knew Zac had just released it the morning before. Apparently, almost half the town had come over and scrubbed, fixing broken things or replacing that which couldn't be repaired. There were a few baby-related items that looked really familiar and she finally realized they were the shower gifts she'd been looking for. She found out Anthony had dumped them all at the resale store. The woman who ran the place had been to the shower, recognized everything, and immediately boxed it all up to return to Olivia.

Olivia could recall Anthony's derision of "worthless junk," and fought a stab of anger. There wasn't much point in being annoyed at his callous attitude now.

She moved to what used to be her bedroom and glanced through the doorway. In place of the queen-size bed there were four wicker bassinets lined up against an interior wall for warmth. They didn't match—they'd been gathered by the people of Westerly in record time—but they were clean and met every safety standard and Olivia was profoundly grateful. Tanks of oxygen were stacked against the wall while the soft hum of machinery and monitors filled the air. The rest of the room was filled with two changing tables, two rockers, two dressers as well as her old armoire only now Anthony's mother's figurines shared the top shelf with her father's ditty box. The armoire itself was stuffed with stacks of diapers instead of Olivia's winter clothes.

Her sister Sandy sat in a rocking chair, a baby against her shoulder, both of them apparently sound asleep. Faith stood over a bassinet. As Olivia moved, Faith met her gaze and put a finger against her lips. She tiptoed to meet Olivia and both women adjourned to the living room.

"They're all asleep at the same time," Faith said with a sense of wonder.

"It's a miracle," Olivia said.

"According to Sandy's chart, no one should wake up hungry for at least an hour. I'm going to hang out on the couch, you probably saw that Sandy fell asleep in the rocking chair with Jillian. They both looked comfy so I left them alone. You better catch a little sleep while you can. Where's Zac?"

"He's upstairs putting my office back together."

"Go get some sleep," Faith said in that voice of hers.

"Okay."

Faith smiled as she disappeared toward the house's one bathroom. Olivia glanced down the hall toward the small back room that was technically hers now, but she knew she couldn't sleep. There was way too much on her mind. She thought of taking a walk, but the day had grown colder, the rain was falling with conviction. She decided to see how Zac was getting on in the turret office.

She found him sitting at her desk amid a sea of paper, staring out the window. He apparently hadn't heard her come up the stairs.

He looked almost as tired as she felt, but he seemed to sense her presence and looked up, his lips curving into a smile when he saw her. He started to get to his feet.

"Sit," she said, brushing papers off the office futon and gingerly perching on the edge. The C-section site hurt today, and climbing the stairs hadn't helped any. She'd always been athletic, had jogged miles until the doctor strictly forbid it because of the fact she was carrying four babies, but face it, the last couple of months had been grueling.

They talked about babies and schedules for a few moments—it was the topic de rigueur in the house—but Olivia could tell Zac had something else on his mind. She touched his arm. "What's going on, Zac? Get it out."

He stared at her fingers, his deep-blue eyes uneasy when he finally lifted his gaze to hers. "The bank has frozen your assets."

"My assets. You mean Anthony's?"

"You were married. Everything is frozen."

She rubbed her forehead. "Great."

"Anthony was screwing around with other people's money. As I understand it—and trust me, it gets confusing—he convinced the Robinson brothers and a couple of other investors in Seattle to back the ski equipment business we all heard about, then using that support, obtained accounts and loans at a couple of financial institutions. Then he got a bank to fund a string of exclusive northwest inns. The construction out on the point was the prototype. The bank and contractors had no idea he'd told you it was a private residence. He told them he was in the process of getting a permit to dredge a small marina—"

"He lied to everyone," she said.

"Hold on, it gets worse. He then apparently

diverted money to who knows where, probably himself, probably under a new identity in a different state which begs the question, is he really Anthony Capri?"

Olivia sat back on the futon and made a conscious effort to close her mouth. Why had this man married her? Who was he? Had anything she thought she loved about him actually existed? Had he really been a pilot or played in the Super Bowl or deep-sea dived or made his grub stake by investing in Midas Touch?

"Bank and investment fraud are federal charges," Zac said gently. "It's all messed up now because of Anthony's death. That's why you don't have any of that baby equipment that was delivered to the place out on the point. You used a credit card he gave you and everything is frozen. It'll all have to go back."

"I guess it's a good thing I don't own this house," she mumbled.

"If you did it could end up with everything else. The bank is anticipating multiple lawsuits."

"And as his wife, I'm legally responsible for his finances?"

"I'm not sure. You're going to want to talk to a lawyer."

"When I think about the hospital bills alone—"

"I know."

"Have you talked to the Robinsons yet?"

"No. They left town kind of suddenly. Dilly is looking under every rock trying to find them. So far, no luck."

"They ran?" She clasped her hands together, trembling inside. She'd known the Robinson brothers most of her life. They'd been contemporaries of her father. Though her father's wealth had been mostly on paper, the Robinsons were old-money rich and the fact they'd suddenly left town struck her as ominous. It wasn't hard to picture either man striking out at Anthony—they might be twenty years older than he but they were both healthy and Grant had a temper. But it was next to impossible to imagine them ransacking her house or burying Anthony in a garage.

"I think they got wind folks were talking about them and decided to sit it out."

"I can't believe any of this is happening," Olivia said.

"It's all pretty crazy, I agree. Listen, Olivia, if you need money—"

"No, I'll figure out the money. I've worked my whole life. I can go back to work."

"You are at work," he said. "You have four infants to care for and that's going to get expensive."

"Well, let's see. Anthony paid for the car outright and it's in my name, my maiden name, I believe. Maybe I'll be able to keep that and sell it. And how about my engagement ring? I know he paid a small fortune for it and that was a gift to me before we were married."

"You need to see a lawyer."

"Yeah."

"There's something else," he said. "I haven't wanted to frighten you, but you have to keep in mind that Anthony was a crook and that puts a whole new spin on the break-in of your house before he died."

"What do you mean?"

"I think someone was looking for something valuable. I'm not convinced Anthony turned it over. Because his car was here but his body was out at the other house, it kind of looks to me like he tried to con that someone into thinking he had hidden something out there. We'll keep looking, but you need to stay alert. It's possible that whoever did this will come back."

"I know. You told me all this at the hospital. I'm not going to be run out of my house."

"Well, I have deputies checking out your street day and night."

"I don't know what I'd do without you and Faith," Olivia said.

He smiled, kind of, but not really. She wasn't sure why he looked so thoughtful as he glanced away from her face and stared down at his boots.

He'd abandoned the city suits for the tan Westerly uniform and on his lean frame and with his dark hair, it looked good. He looked good.

"I don't know why you're being so nice to me," she added. "By all rights, you should be singing I told you so. You tried to warn me about Anthony, but I wouldn't listen. If I hadn't been so damn stubborn—"

"You wouldn't have those babies down there," Zac said.

She nodded. Less than a week and already they defined the parameters of her life. "Do you ever wish you and Lynn had had children?"

"I never used to, but lately, yeah, I kind of wish we had. She mentioned it during our ill-fated marriage but I wasn't ready." He shook his head and added, "Talk about water under the bridge."

This was one of the very few conversations they'd had where Zac revealed anything personal and Olivia was poised to ask additional questions. For one thing, it was a relief to focus on someone else's life for a change. Her plans were cut short when his phone rang.

She tensed as his voice became guarded and he turned his back to her. What now? What more could go wrong? Oh, come on, reason alone said things were bound to get worse before they got better. For instance, what if they knew who killed Anthony and it was someone she knew or loved? Or, worse, what if it was a nameless, faceless stranger who had one thing on the brain and that was coming back to this house?

She hugged herself as Zac pocketed his phone and got to his feet. He extended a hand and she took it, grateful for any help when it came to getting up off the low futon. But it was more than that. She was spooked and his warm hand just made her feel better. He set the other hand atop her shoulder and said, "You're shaking."

"It's been a very long last few days. Who was that on the phone?"

"Dilly got a lead. Seems the Robinson brothers have retreated to their cabin. I'm going to go meet him at the station and drive out there to question them."

She nodded as she fought the urge to ask him to stay right where he was. She had no right to ask something like that of him. He was already doing more than he probably should.

"I'll swing by in a couple of hours when I get back to town," he said. He stared at her a long time before adding, "Popular opinion aside, I have a hard time believing Grant or Hugh killed your husband. Keep the doors locked, okay?"

"Okay," she said as a warm tear slid down her face.

He caught it on his fingertip. "Hey, I thought you didn't cry."

"I don't. It's hormones. I have too many of them. They're running amok."

"I know the feeling," he said, and dipping his head, kissed her cheek.

She stood looking after him, her fingers against the place on her skin where his lips had touched.

Beneath the layer of fear kindled by Zac's warnings, another feeling tried to break through.

She pushed it away.

Chapter Five

Hugh and Grant Robinson were sixty and sixty-two years old respectively. Hugh had never married, Grant had married once for about twelve minutes. They shared the big old mansion on Main Street they'd grown up in, but they also had cabins and houses spread all over the state of Washington and into Idaho and Montana. On this occasion, apparently, they'd decided on visiting the one closest to Westerly, making it unlikely they were using it as a hideout.

More likely, they just got tired of the gossip.

Zac and Dilly leaned against their big red truck parked out front of the dilapidated cabin and looked at the tires.

Dilly swore softly. "Could be the same size and tread, I'm not sure. We got a lab working on what kind of tire we're looking for. Sure would like to take a cast of these."

"Did you bring the dental stone?"

"In the trunk."

"Let's talk to the boys first," Zac said. "If they don't cooperate, we'll get a court order."

"I'll go around back, just in case they try to escape," Dilly said. They'd parked the sheriff's car at the bottom of the drive and hiked in. No reason to go out of their way to announce their arrival.

Zac nodded and Dilly disappeared around the cabin. The fog had moved back in, hanging low just above the ground. Cold and damp, maybe, but it made sneaking around easier. Still, Zac wished he'd brought a jacket as he decided on a frontal approach with no weapon drawn. He walked up the rickety stairs and pounded on the door.

"That you, Bishop?" one of the brothers called from inside.

So much for a sneaky approach. He should have known there was a surveillance camera on the front door. "Yeah, it's me. It's cold out here."

The door opened. Grant Robinson stood there, thinning blond hair uncombed as usual, wearing a red-and-blue flannel shirt and black suspenders, holding a brown bottle of microbrew. Behind him, Zac could see Hugh sitting in one of two leather recliners facing a hearth. A bright fire danced on the grate. The cabin was homey inside, belying its ratty exterior.

"We didn't hear a car," Grant said.

"I decided a walk would do me good," Zac said, shaking Grant's baseball mitt–size hand.

Hugh put his coffee cup down on the table by his side. He was smaller than his brother though not by much, and often affected an urban air. Zac glanced down at both men's feet. They both looked like they wore a size twelve. "I thought I saw Dilly slip by the window a second ago. Grant, you better go let him in the back door. Careful he doesn't shoot you."

Both brothers laughed as Zac crossed the room and shook Hugh's offered hand.

"I heard you took the job of sheriff when old Knotts got caught stealing from the evidence room," Hugh said. "Congratulations. I'm glad you're back in Westerly." He was dressed as differently from his informal brother as could be, wearing chinos and a perfectly ironed long-sleeve button-down shirt. If Grant evoked the image of a lumberjack, Hugh looked and acted like a relaxed college professor.

"I need to ask you and Grant where you were last Monday," Zac said as Grant came back into the room followed by a sheepish looking Dilly.

"We was at home," Grant said. He picked his beer up from where he'd set the bottle on the hearth, took a swig and glared at Zac, daring him to doubt it.

Zac said, "Anyone see you there?"

"I saw Hugh, Hugh saw me," Grant said. "We was

working a 3-D puzzle thing our niece gave us. Hell of a thing. Looks like Windsor Castle. Who'd give a couple of old bachelors something like that?"

"I thought it was delightful," Hugh said.

"You would."

"Back to Monday," Zac said. "Neither one of you left the house?"

"Nope. We did the damn puzzle and then we made burgers. I drank three beers. Hugh had a glass of white wine. We watched some TV and went to bed."

"You mind if we take casts of your truck tires?" Dilly asked.

Grant set the bottle on the mantle so hard Zac thought for sure it would crack. "I sure as hell do mind. Just because that con man screwed us out of a couple million bucks, you think we killed him? Everyone in town is talking about us behind our backs. I've half a mind to tell my lawyer to sue the county—"

Hugh interrupted his brother's tirade. "Wouldn't it just be quicker and simpler to let them cast the tires?" Glancing at Dilly, he added, "Do the sedan in the garage at our house while you're at it. Do the ATVs. Do the bikes. Hell, cast every tire you can find, we have nothing to hide."

"You know what?" Grant fumed. "I wish I had

thought of killing Capri." He jammed both his hands in his pockets and glared at Zac.

Hugh said, "You don't mean that, Grant. Think about poor little Olivia. All those babies and now no husband."

"She's better off without that jerk," Grant said. "Man was a lying no-good scheming lowlife."

"Now, that's true, you're right about that," Hugh said.

Zac didn't say anything, but he had to agree.

Grant added, "Besides, for all we know, Olivia was in it with him."

Zac looked Grant straight in the eye. "Don't say things like that."

"I can speak my mind—"

"Not about her, not like that and not to me."

Grant shook his head, but at least he shut his mouth.

THE NEXT FEEDING went surprisingly well, although that was undoubtedly because three women from the hardware store where Olivia did the books came to offer assistance. They promised to come back the next day. It was all Olivia could do not to kiss them.

Between fending off reporters who called or even came to the door, getting bottles ready, feeding, changing diapers, burping, cleaning up after spit ups and rocking back to sleep, the hours flew by. When Olivia heard a knock on the door she was sure it was Zac and her heart unexpectedly leaped in her chest. Sandy was asleep on the lumpy futon upstairs and Faith had sacked out on Olivia's bed. Olivia had sent her mother home to get some decent rest, Megan was off with a boyfriend and Tabitha was at a junior college event.

She slipped the baby monitor in her pocket, thinking maybe Zac would have time to take a quick walk, and glanced out the window to make sure there wasn't a news van parked at the curb. A man walked under the streetlight in the front of the house headed north, a long jacket pulled up tight around his neck as though he was cold. She didn't care. The thought of fresh air—even dark, cold fresh air—sounded heavenly and if that guy could handle the chill, so could she and Zac. She grabbed her coat off the back of the chair and opened the door.

Three men stood on her small front porch, lit dimly by an inadequate bulb. She couldn't place any of them. Her first reaction was to slam the door in their faces, but she'd opened it too far in anticipation of Zac, and one had braced his arm against the wood behind her, raising more alarm bells.

"Mrs. Capri?" the tallest one asked. They stood in descending order of height. The one who spoke was tall, bulky and dark with a high forehead and a sloping nose. The middle one was thinner, sandier, coarser. The shortest one was bald and didn't seem to have any eyebrows. He was pasty white as though he avoided the sun. They all wore dark overcoats.

Maybe they were newsmen. Maybe they were irate investors. Warily, she said, "What can I do for you?"

"We came to talk to you about your husband," the short one said.

"I am not giving interviews—"

With lightning speed, the short man grabbed her hand and tugged her out onto the porch. The tall man seized her from the back, covering her mouth with a cloth held in his hand, while the middle one quietly closed the front door.

The tall one spoke into her ear. "If you scream, someone inside that house will come to your aid, right?"

She looked across the street, hoping the walker she'd spied a few minutes earlier might still be around, but the street was deserted. She nodded vigorously.

"And when they do, Shorty will give them an introduction to his knife. Show it to her, Shorty."

Shorty flipped his coat aside to reveal a generous flash of steel, covered again at once.

"So, I'm going to let go of you and you're going

to answer a couple of questions and do as we ask and then we'll go away, okay?"

She nodded again, praying Faith or Sandy didn't wake up and come looking for her. The tall man withdrew his hand and turned to face her.

"We saw on the television this morning that your husband passed away. We're sorry about that."

She waited.

"'Course we knew your husband by the name of Gray. Paul Gray."

"The name he used in Seattle," she whispered.

"That's right. But a couple of nights ago we caught the press conference. Your mother held up his photo so we know he was really Anthony Capri."

"What do you want?"

"The man we work for, our boss, you could say, well he sent us to ask you real nicely to cover your late husband's debt."

"He owes the boss fifty thousand dollars," the middle man said. He had a low, throaty voice, like he'd been drinking rot gut straight from a bottle for thirty years.

Olivia looked from one to the other. These men frightened her but there were some basic truths that were unavoidable. "My husband owed everyone money," she said. "I'm afraid your boss will have to get in line. I'm going to see a lawyer as soon as I can get an appointment. If you leave me your names and how I can reach you, I'll let you know what she suggests you do to make a claim against the bank or however that works."

All three men laughed in varying degrees of intensity from a hoarse bark to a high-pitched giggle.

"No, ma'am," the tall man said, "you don't understand. We don't collect money from banks. Show her the note, Shorty."

This time Shorty produced a handwritten promissory note with Anthony's signature—or at least his handwriting. She recognized his confident sprawl. He'd signed it Paul Gray.

"The boss won this money from him fair and square and he wants it. Now."

"What do you mean he won it? How?"

"Poker," the tall man said. "Just a few friendly games is all. After a run of good luck, your husband suffered a couple of losing streaks. He paid up once before, we're sure he would have paid off again only he got killed."

"Well, I'm sorry, but I don't have that kind of money. I don't have any money, truth be known."

"Yeah, well, see, we heard you on that interview. You said you and your hubby didn't have no secrets from each other, that you were partners."

"That's really nice," Shorty said. "Especially now that he's dead. He paid off debts to the boss before by fencing something and since he got killed here, we figure that something is here, too."

"My husband wasn't killed at this house," Olivia said. A sense of unreality had begun to settle.

"You're splitting hairs, lady. Anyway, all you have to do is do what he did."

"What he did? I don't know what you're talking about."

"Go get more of whatever it was he fenced the first time and pay the boss," the tall man said patiently. "Otherwise, someone you love is going to meet Shorty's knife in a very unpleasant way."

Acid seemed to creep up Olivia's throat. Had these men followed Anthony home, had they killed him? She scanned the empty street wishing Zac would hurry. What was to keep them from overpowering her and going inside?

"We could just walk in there and take one or two of her kids," Middle Guy said as though he'd read Olivia's mind. "I bet that would jog her memory."

"This is insane," Olivia said. "I haven't forgotten anything. I don't know what you're talking about."

A car turned the far corner, the headlights sweeping the street. Olivia willed it to be Zac. The three men reacted to her focused concentration on the approaching vehicle by stepping down off the porch, the tall one lingering a second as the car rolled on by. Olivia recognized an elderly neighbor, but another car turned the same corner a second later and she watched the approaching headlights, her heart slamming against her ribs. Olivia was sure she'd spied a light rack on the roof when the car passed beneath the street lamp.

She said, "You people better leave. I'm expecting the sheriff. And don't come back. I can't help you."

The tall man said, "This is between you and us. You got twenty-four hours, lady. Remember what I said about someone you love and Shorty's knife. And I should add, there ain't nowhere you can go that we can't find you."

As one, they all turned, their dark coats flapping to the sides like crows' wings, and almost swooped to the curb. They got into a low, black car, two men in the front seat, Shorty in back, and pulled away from the curb. Olivia stepped off the porch, peering after them, looking for a license plate number, but the light in the back by the plate had burned out. The car Olivia had thought might be Zac's kept going by her house.

Shaking deep inside, she swore violently. "Oh, Anthony, you S.O.B., what did you do? What have you gotten us into?"

OLIVIA WAS STANDING in her driveway under a light, a slight figure in a blue wool coat, backed up to the closed garage door as though shielding her back. Her ebony hair tumbled onto her shoulders, her complexion glowed like new snow.

She held a baby monitor in one hand and the coat closed with the other giving the impression she didn't have the wherewithal to fasten the buttons.

Zac's stomach tightened into a knot as he pulled up next to her. She was in his arms the moment he got out of the car, her body shaking, soft strangled noises coming from her throat. Holding her tenderly, he spoke against her hair. "Shh, honey, what's wrong?"

It took her a few moments to regain her composure, and when she did, she threw him an embarrassed glance. "They just left, not five minutes ago. I got so spooked, Zac. Damn, damn, I'm crying again."

"It doesn't matter," he said, finding his handkerchief and passing it to her. He'd just started carrying one a few weeks before which struck him as a stroke of good luck. "Tell me what happened. Who left?"

He coaxed her toward the door, but she sat on the back stoop as though loathe to take her anxiety into the house where it might affect her children. The story she related sounded like something out of a book. When she got to the part about Shorty and his knife he noticed she'd all but stopped breathing.

She could give him no license plate number, but

he called the description into the station anyway, asking all on duty officers be on the lookout for a dark sedan with burned out lights next to the rear license plate.

"What has Anthony done to us?" she said as he flipped off his phone. "Gambling? Is that it? Is that where all his money went?"

"I don't know," Zac said. "I've heard rumors about a couple of high-stake clubs with strong-arm measures for losers who don't pay up but it wasn't my beat so I don't know the details. I can get them, though."

"So maybe they followed him down here and tore apart my house and then killed him?"

"That would be like killing the goose that laid the golden egg. But maybe if he lied often enough and tried to cheat one of them things got out of hand. So, these guys think you're still in possession of whatever it was Anthony fenced?"

"Yes. They're going to come back tomorrow. Oh, Zac." She turned stricken eyes from him to the house to the street, to the heavens as though looking for some venue of escape.

"Pack up the kids and yourself, you can come home with me right now—"

"No, Zac. I can't do that. It took everyone hours to get settled here, I can't pick up this late in the day. Isn't there another way, at least until morning?"

He took her hands in his. "They've connected you with the treasure, whatever it is. And you're connected with this house."

"I have four brand-new infants. Everyone in this town knows when I take a deep breath. Half of the citizens are signed up to help with round the clock feedings. If I move to your place, everyone will know, even those horrible men. They warned me they would know. They'll just come after me. They'll come after all of us."

He studied her face for a few moments. They'd given her twenty-four hours. Surely he could guard the house for that long and maybe come up with a plan to entrap them. He said, "Deputy Hoopes' wife teaches art at the junior college. We've used her before. You describe these jokers, Sara will make sketches and I'll fax them to Seattle to my former partner, see what he can find out. Meanwhile, we'll create a trap here tomorrow night for these losers. You'll have to agree to take your children away for a few hours—"

"Anything."

"Okay. We'll try it. But first I keep thinking about those boxes of Anthony's, the ones down in the basement. Do you know what's in them?"

"No, we never really talked about them. I just figured it was family stuff. I mean, all his relatives are dead. Whoever searched the house didn't get down to the basement so maybe you're right."

"Maybe that's why Anthony led them away from here. Maybe he wanted to get them out of the house before they got down there. With his ego, he probably thought he could out trick them in the end."

As soon as the words left his mouth he regretted them. He'd been thinking out loud, he hadn't used his head. The last thing he wanted to do was force her into sticking up for this scum ball. He prepared himself to be chastised.

"Yeah," she said, standing up. "Of course, who knows what he really was."

"About that. The Feds are checking out his identity, tracing him. You need to be prepared…"

She held up a hand. "When you know, just tell me who I'm burying, okay?"

"Uh, actually you aren't burying anyone, at least not until his body is released," Zac said. "Damn, I was supposed to tell you earlier today—"

"It doesn't matter, Zac. I'm not exactly planning a big gathering. It's kind of hard given the circumstances."

"Maybe by the weekend—"

"Whatever. Okay, let's go tear apart those boxes."

She still looked awfully pale to him, her eyes were ringed in dark circles and she held herself as though the act of changing from a sitting position to a standing one hurt. He wanted to tuck her away somewhere safe, he wanted to make things easier for her, but he didn't know how. She was a grown woman with some very real problems and responsibilities. That they felt like his problems too was information she probably wouldn't want to hear. She was leaning on him for support, but he wasn't going to kid himself into thinking it was anything more than that.

"I could get started while you catch a little sleep," he said.

"Sleep, what's sleep?" she mumbled as they climbed the stairs. The moment her hand touched the knob, she turned to him. He'd been pretty close behind her so they were more or less nose to nose. "What about the Robinson brothers?"

"Hard to say," he told her, searching her eyes. For what, some sign that she thought of him as more than a steadfast friend?

"Did they have alibis?"

"Sort of. They alibied each other. Dilly is over at their house right now taking casts of their car tires. He'll check out their closets, too, look at their shoes, though if they put him off we'll need a warrant. He already got the truck."

"And they agreed to that?"

"Grant grumbled, Hugh insisted."

"Grant grumbles about everything, but if Hugh insisted it must mean neither one of them had anything to do with it. That's a relief. It must be those horrible gamblers."

"Yeah, well, I hate to burst your bubble, but if Hugh or Grant or both of them are guilty, insisting we check their tires is exactly what they'd do. If we find a match for the tire track out at the point, they'll just come up with an explanation for why it's there. Mud on their shoes, imprints that match our footprint, ditto. They were business partners, they were looking for Anthony, this time of year, as much rain as we've had, who knows how long the impressions have been around?"

"Then what did you learn by talking to them?"

Zac shrugged. "We learned neither one of them have an alibi for Monday and they both hated Anthony Capri."

"Still, I'm betting on these gamblers."

"Just don't jump to conclusions. The Robinson brothers decided to come back into town so they could watch Dilly do his job. I don't want them anywhere near you, okay?"

"But—"

"Olivia? These men tonight are a wild card. They could be sleaze-ball enforcers who had nothing to do with Anthony's death or they could be murderers. Same goes for Hugh and Grant. I'm just asking you to stay alert."

She nodded once and he was sorry to watch more fear creep into her eyes.

"How about this little painting?" Olivia said an hour later. They'd eaten dinner—a pizza Faith called out for—and were now sitting on the comfortable chairs Anthony had set up in the basement. Olivia wondered if the furniture store would be reclaiming them or if the bank would foreclose on things she didn't even know her name was on. The legal hassles looming ahead were more than she could stand to think about.

Zac took the small painting from her. No more than ten by twelve inches and framed in gilded wood, it looked valuable. They couldn't read the artist's name, but the strokes were bold, the colors rich. The picture itself depicted a stormy sky and a small huddled group of buildings beneath.

"We'll need an appraiser," Zac said. "There's a book of stamps in here, too, plus a bag of old coins that might be worth something."

"And baseball cards," Olivia said. "This is like that old movie, the one where everyone is looking for a dead man's fortune and all the time it's the rare stamp on a postcard."

Zac's phone rang. Olivia dropped the cards back

in the box from which she'd taken them and leaned back in the chair, closing her eyes as Zac's voice filled her head. It was hard to recall the months they hadn't been friends, they were almost like a dream…

The next thing she knew, Zac was leaning over her, covering her with a blanket. The room was darker, only the lit stairway illuminating a pie-shaped wedge of the basement.

Apparently seeing her open eyes, he knelt by her side. "I have to go for a while, Olivia. There's been a traffic accident out at the overpass. Faith told me to tell you she and your sisters are taking care of this feeding. You just stay here and catch some sleep. They'll come get you if they need you."

She nodded. His words were lost almost as soon as he uttered them, but the deep calm of his voice and nearness of his face to hers was not. She reached up and touched his cheek, barely aware of the sudden stillness that wrapped itself around them both.

"You kissed me once, remember?" she whispered, closing her eyes.

It took him a moment to answer and then it was a simple, "I remember."

"I was seventeen. I had such a crush on you."

"And I should have known better than to take advantage of you," he said softly, but he'd leaned into her fingers, his warm breath caressing her face, his lips against the tender pads of her fingers.

"Kiss me again," she murmured.

This time the pause was even longer, and then there were no words, just the incredibly hot, soft feel of his mouth closing on hers.

Oh, the delicious warmth of that kiss, the way it flowed through her body, the way it found abandoned niches and flooded them with light, the way it thawed parts of her heart that must have been frozen…

He pulled away at last. She opened her eyes to find him staring down at her, his gaze absolutely unfathomable and yet she got the uneasy feeling she'd crossed a line with him, she'd made a mistake. Reaching for his hand, she murmured, "I'm sorry…"

"Go back to sleep," he said, catching her hand, raising it to his lips and kissing her fingers, then carefully settling her hand back atop her chest and tucking the blankets around her legs before standing up. "I'll be back soon."

She nodded, her eyes already closing again.

THE NEXT TIME she awoke, the room was cold and absolutely pitch-black.

And in a sixth-sense prick of clarity, Olivia knew she wasn't alone.

Chapter Six

As Olivia's heartbeat thudded in her ears, several impressions imprinted themselves simultaneously on her brain.

The basement door must be wide open for it was from that direction a thin, cold wind blew into the room.

A big dark shape hovered near the pile of boxes. Too bulky for Zac, too tall for most women. A man whose movements were slow and deliberate, watchful, cautious. This person was slowly but surely moving boxes around. How she knew this fact, she wasn't sure. Maybe she heard sounds—whatever, he was moving boxes.

There was no light in the room, not from the stairs, not from the outside light in the driveway, or from the nightlight in the corner. Not even the little green light on the satellite receiver glowed. That meant the electricity was out. If she was right, it also meant the babies were without their equipment in a house that would do nothing but get colder.

Now she had a decision to make. Scream? Faith or one of her sisters would come running. What would happen to them when they tripped blindly down those stairs? If this was the biggest of the gamblers, were the rest of them already inside the house? Was Shorty there with his knife?

Her babies!

Should she try to escape out the basement door? Could she move past the intruder without being seen? If her children were in danger, this might be her one chance to get to them and she couldn't blow it. Was it possible the intruder didn't even know she was in that chair under the blanket? If he had cut the electricity line before entering, perhaps he didn't.

Maybe she should make a noise of some kind to alert him she was there and give him an opportunity to run away. If he was alone that ought to work.

Caught in an indecisive hellhole, she saw a flash-light blink on. The beam traveled over the contents of the boxes for several seconds as though the man holding it was studying what he saw, and then it suddenly flicked toward Olivia's chair and went out.

He knew she was there.

Olivia finally made a decision. She would try to get to the back door unobserved. For better or worse, she couldn't lie there another moment. In the second she slowly made the first move to disentangle herself from the blanket tucked around her legs, she heard a man's muted voice come from upstairs. It sounded like he was outside the front door. Pounding soon followed. As the door was located directly opposite the stairs leading to the basement, the racket thundered down the stairwell.

This was followed by more voices, female this time, Sandy's maybe or Megan's, then the faint cries of babies, more pounding, all as Olivia folded back the blanket and tried to get to her feet without drawing attention to herself. She could tell the intruder had turned to look up the stairs but he must have caught some sense of her movement. As Olivia stood, the man ran at her, landing a blow to her cheek with what felt like the end of the flashlight. She cried out. The wallop also whipped her around and she fell back against the small table and lamp beside the chair, crashing to the floor in an unholy heap, screaming as she clutched her face, the pain in her abdomen bursting into flame.

The intruder kept on going toward the door, which slammed decisively a moment later. At the same time someone grabbed her arms and she lashed out.

"It's me!" Zac yelled as she struggled to free herself.

She stopped fighting as he hauled her to her feet. It was still too dark to see much though the open door at the top of the stairs must have admitted enough light to turn things from black to deep gray. "Are you hurt? What happened? Is that blood?"

The questions came fast and furious as did her responses. "There was a man in here. He came and left through the basement door. What about upstairs, what about the babies? Are my sisters and Faith okay?"

She'd torn away from Zac as she spoke, stumbling toward the stairs, feeling with outstretched hands to find the stair railing, the shadowy light filtering down the stairs like a beacon. She hurt like crazy. Her incision site hurt, her face throbbed, but all that paled next to the thought of what could have happened upstairs in the minutes she lay in that chair riddled with indecision.

She tripped on the bottom step and fell back against Zac. A wave of dizziness made her breath catch.

"We've got to get the electricity back on," he said.

"Are you guys okay down there?" Faith called from upstairs. A second later, the beam of a flashlight fell on Olivia's face. Faith screamed. "Oh, my God, Olivia! You're hurt."

"I'm okay," Olivia said, pulling herself up the narrow stairs, though her hand, covered with blood from her face, slipped on the railing. "What about the babies? Are the rest of you—"

"Everyone up here is fine," Faith said, coming down a few steps to offer Olivia additional support. "Zac started pounding on the door and woke us all up. I didn't even know the electricity was off until then."

"You didn't leave the children alone—"

"No, no, Sandy is in with them, Megan and Tabitha went home an hour or so ago. I guess the wind blew a tree into a pole—"

"No, it's just this house," Zac said. "A deputy called it in and I raced over here."

"There was someone in the basement," Olivia said. "I have to see my babies."

"Honey," Faith said, "you can't touch them until you wash up. You're covered in blood." She flashed the light over Olivia's hands. Bright red streaks ran down her arms, covered her blouse. "You need stitches," Faith said.

"Sandy can help me. She's a nurse," Olivia said.

She saw the way Faith and Zac exchanged glances. Another flashlight showed up at the front door, this one held by a man wearing a jacket with the electric company logo on the pocket. "We got a call," he said. "Looks like someone cut your lines."

"I'll take care of this," Zac told Olivia.

"Do you want your flashlight back?" Faith said.

"No, you keep it, I'll grab another out of the trunk."

Olivia heard this exchange as she made her way across the living room in the shadows thrown by the lights, anxious to get to the nursery.

Sandy had used the cross beams of two more flashlights to illuminate as much of the room as possible. Without the hum of machines, it was eerily silent, but then Olivia heard a gurgle and a coo and her heart seemed to start beating again. She walked to the nearest bassinet, but Sandy caught her before she could touch Antoinette. "Stop right there, Olivia. Antoinette is fine, you're a mess. Come on into the bathroom and I'll help you."

From the doorway, Faith said, "Don't worry, I'll stay right here until you come back."

Olivia allowed herself to be led to the bathroom where a brief glance at her face in the mirror lit by a newly found battery operated lantern made her stomach lurch. The gash on her face was two inches long and sliced across her left cheekbone. Sandy expertly washed and applied bandages, murmuring to herself that it was superficial, more blood than damage. Afterward, Olivia washed up and changed clothes. Within a half hour, she was back with the babies in their room, sitting in a rocking chair cradling two of them while the other two were held by Faith and Sandy respectively. A half hour after that, the lights came on.

THEY TOOK separate cars to the station because Olivia refused to risk any chance she might become stranded away from home. Zac had no option but to agree to this, though he did follow right on her bumper. He'd also diverted a deputy to stand guard outside her house and was relieved when Olivia's mother and other sisters came to stay with the babies. Faith was taking a much earned day off doing laundry and catching up on her sleep.

Zac was finding it hard to forgive himself for not being with Olivia when she needed him, and seeing her black-and-blue eye and bandaged cheek didn't help matters. He knew she'd spent the rest of the night standing guard in the babies' room, even though he'd insisted on staying at her house. He couldn't blame her. Within a week she'd gone from being a married pregnant woman to a widowed mother with four infants. Her life must seem like it was falling to pieces.

He'd been called to an accident out at the overpass that had claimed two teenage lives and destroyed three cars, an unholy mess, equal parts blood and booze. They'd all gotten so wrapped up in it and the ensuing traffic snarl that the patrol on

Olivia's house had been unintentionally put on hold. As long as he lived, Zac would never forget that call telling him Olivia's house was the only dark one on her street or him pounding on her front door, shoving his flashlight at a terrified Faith and running down those black stairs to find Olivia tangled in blankets, furniture and a lamp cord.

Sara Hoopes met them at the station and after doing a double take when she saw Olivia's battered face, settled down to try to coax her into remembering the faces of the men who had visited the evening before. Zac could tell it was frustrating for both women—these things were always more difficult than a person thought they would be.

He left them alone as Sara sketched, the backlog of work on his own desk mind-boggling, and more than a little of it centered around Anthony Capri. He also took a call from his old partner in Seattle who he'd spoken to the night before. Before Zac could warn him to be on the look out for the pictures, he learned why his partner had called.

Zac needed to come to Seattle to give testimony on a case he worked on while he was a cop there. They wanted him tomorrow morning. Tomorrow. Dave also mentioned getting together to talk about Anthony Capri.

Did he dare leave Westerly? Well, if they trapped the gamblers tonight and kept a close eye on the

Robinson brothers, it should be okay. Nevertheless, there was something else he needed to do that day that took number one priority, and that was make sure Olivia's house was secure.

He called Dilly into his office and asked him to see Olivia back to her place and keep someone on the door until further notice, then he walked down the hall and peeked into the room where Sara was just finishing up. Olivia sat at the table drinking a cup of high-octane office coffee which meant she wouldn't be taking a nap anytime soon.

"I have a lot of work to do around here so I'm going to get Dilly to follow you home," he said.

She titled her head. "You're spending too much time worrying about me."

He blew off her concern. "I also want to tell you I have a call into that house alarm place down the road. I'm going to have a system installed in your house today."

"I can't afford an alarm system—"

"It's a gift from me to you. Call it a baby gift."

"That's too much—"

"Please," he said.

"I think that's a great idea," Sara Hoopes said with a lingering look at Olivia's face. She handed Zac the sketches, adding her good-byes, explaining there were hungry teenagers at home.

He flipped through the three drawings. Sara had made notes about height and any other characteristics Olivia remembered.

"I'm not sure I got any of their faces right," Olivia said as she got to her feet and tossed the empty cup in the trash can. "The light was poor and I was frightened. Frankly, I had no idea it would be so hard to reconstruct someone. I mean, Sara wanted to know if the tall man's eyes were round or almond shape. I don't know, I can't remember. How about his hair? Thick or thinning? Thinning, I think, but that's just it, I can't remember for sure. Did the middle-size man have any distinguishing characteristics, a scar perhaps, a mole? Was Shorty heavyset, did he have bushy eyebrows, was his nose broad or flat or narrow or large? I thought I was observant, but apparently, not so much."

"You're not the first eyewitness to have this trouble. We can get some mug shots put together for you to look at, too. Do you think any of these three might have been the guy in the basement?"

"Maybe the tallest—I don't know."

"Whoever he was, he apparently wore gloves. There were no unaccounted for fingerprints downstairs."

"Figures."

"And the door was opened by someone breaking

one of the glass panes by the lock and reaching in. I don't how you slept through it, except you were so exhausted."

"That's how. Zac, about this alarm…"

"Please don't argue with me."

"I'm not going to. I just want to say thanks. For everything, I mean."

He smiled wistfully, amazed she could be so unaware of his feelings for her. *And whose fault is that?* a tiny voice whispered in his ear. He told the voice to shut up. "Do you have somewhere to take the babies tonight?"

"I'm taking them to my mother's house. Between her and me and my three sisters, there'll be plenty of us. I told Faith to stay away until I called her. She's home catching some well-earned sleep."

"It sounds like you have a plan."

"We have a doctor's appointment for Brianna, then we'll all go to Mom's house. Don't look worried, Brianna is fine. It's just a checkup, starting with her first because she's the smallest."

"Dilly will follow you home now—"

"That's not necessary—"

"Sure, it is." He stared at her a second longer, wondering if she recalled their kiss the night before. She'd been half-asleep and then she'd apologized. What he wouldn't give for the right to wrap her in his arms, to insist she follow his directions. He had the horrible, sick feeling that she would never be his, that when this crisis was over, she'd move on with her life. And somewhere deep inside himself he knew that he was looking at the one woman he was put on earth to love and that when he lost her again, it would be for the last time.

So, he couldn't lose her. He would get her through this and then he would make her love him.

"Zac, what's wrong?"

"I guess I'm a little tired, too," he said.

"We're all tired. When this is over, I plan to sleep for a week."

"Do you think your little pink tyrants will allow that?"

She smiled again. "They are adorable, aren't they? I'm beginning to be able to tell them apart even without looking at the toenail polish. Brianna is a little smaller than the others, Antoinette's face is a little rounder, Jillian is bit longer and Juliet's hair sticks up in front."

"Dare I ask about the toenail polish?"

"I'll show you sometime."

He returned her smile, happy to see her a little more relaxed and enjoying her children.

"I don't know what I'd do if anything happened to one of them," she said, eyes filling up. "I didn't know I could love like this. It's the one good thing Anthony seems to have done with his life."

Zac dug for a clean handkerchief, snatched out of a drawer that morning during his fifteen-minute shower/ change-of-clothes turnaround at home. He'd paid a moving service to pack up his belongings in Seattle and unpack them in Westerly so at least he was no longer living out of a suitcase.

She waved it away. "No, no, thanks, I'm not going to cry. I'm sick of crying."

He tapped the top sketch with a finger. "I'll fax these to my old partner, Dave. Tomorrow I have to drive to Seattle for a meeting."

"Maybe it'll all be over by then," she said.

"I hope so. You be careful—"

"You, too." She looked quickly into his eyes and then away. She was going to have quite a shiner by tomorrow. "I'll wait for Detective Dilly out front, okay?"

"I'll tell him."

He watched her go with a gnawing feeling of foreboding. Damn.

OLIVIA OPENED the station door to find herself face-to-face with Grant Robinson, who was in the process of entering. He'd been one of her father's cronies, but she hadn't seen him since her wedding when the guest list had included just about the whole town—except for Zac. Zac had been invited, but showing up at her house that morning issuing ultimatums and dire warnings had soured both of them for each other's company.

Then he'd moved away and months had gone by, he'd been proven right about Anthony, and she was in a miserable mess.

And Zac grew more important by the hour.

Meanwhile, Grant was bigger than she remembered, ruddier, snarlier. His gaze dwelled on the battered left side of her face and though she could think of no reason he'd break into her house, she still felt a shudder run up her spine.

"Well, well. Olivia."

"Hi, Grant."

"I bet you're wondering what I'm doing here."

She stared at him, unsure how to respond. For one thing, he glowered menacingly and for another his fists were knotted and his chin jutted out. It didn't make sense that he or his brother would be looking for whatever Anthony had that could be fenced. They'd lost millions in investments, not fifty thousand in some undefined goods.

"I'm saving Sheriff Bishop the trouble of coming after me," he volunteered when she failed to respond. "I heard what happened last night. Hell, it's all over town. You can bet Zac Bishop is going to haul me down here and try to blame that incident over at your house on me. Hugh can sit home and wait if he wants, I'm a man of action."

"I'm sorry, Grant—"

"Yeah, well, my daddy used to say sorry don't pay the rent. Me and Hugh lost a bundle because of your husband and I can't say as how I'm too damn upset someone took it in their head to kill the bastard. You might as well know me and Hugh are going to do everything we can to recoup our losses and if that means going after you in court, so be it. You should have known what kind of man you were marrying. I heard you announce to the world how you were his partner. Your father would be ashamed of you."

"Now wait a second—"

Dilly came up behind Olivia just then and she stopped talking as she saw Grant's fists flex.

"What's going on?" Dilly asked.

"Nothing," Olivia said. "Nothing."

"I'm just saving you the bother of coming after me," Grant said. "Of course, I'm going to have trouble finding an alibi for the middle of the night as I was asleep in my own bed."

"Is that so? Sheriff Bishop said he saw you driving around out by the highway in that big red truck of yours."

"That was hours earlier. I heard on my ham radio

there'd been a bad accident out there, wanted to see it for myself."

"So, actually, you weren't home in bed."

"I told you, that was earlier in the evening."

"How about I come out to your place in a little while and talk to you and your brother," Dilly said.

"Hell, no, I want to talk to Bishop. Go to the top, that's my motto."

"Go right ahead," Dilly said, holding the door open for the much bigger man to pass.

"Damn hothead," Dilly said. "Okay, Mrs. Capri, I'll follow you home."

"Just call me Olivia," Olivia said. "Or Ms. Hart if you have to. Anything but Capri."

He laughed. "You got it, Olivia."

She had just left the parking lot when her cell phone rang and she dug it out of her handbag. Her mother had a short list of necessities she wanted Olivia to pick up, all of which were available at the truck stop convenience store which was a lot quicker to get in and out of than the market. Olivia detoured the few blocks toward the main highway, the site of the accident the night before. She imagined Roger Dilly was wondering why she'd veered off this direction.

The only sign there'd been an accident within the past twelve hours was a bent traffic sign and a few mangled bushes. The truck stop was across the road, a big old place built on a couple of acres of land with easy egress. Olivia pulled into one of the few parking spots at the side of the station. The front held the standard gas pumps for autos. The back was much the same only on a larger scale, geared for the long haulers.

Detective Dilly pulled in alongside her. "Is something wrong?" he asked as she stopped at his window.

"I need a few things."

"Want me to go—"

"No, I'm fine. I'll be back in five minutes."

"I'll watch the door," he said. "If you hear me honk, get down low."

She wasn't sure if he was kidding or not.

The place was almost empty, just two guys behind the counter, one eating a doughnut the size of a dinner plate and the other lighting up a cigarette. The smoker did a double take at her appearance—the eye must be going black and blue. Both men looked vaguely familiar as just about everyone who lived or worked in Westerly did.

She snatched a small rolling basket. They needed tissue, milk, juice, soft drinks and baby rice cereal, which Olivia was relieved to find. Reflux, thanks to immature tummies, was a constant problem for the quads and was the reason they added rice cereal to the formula. The soft drinks would be for Tabitha, who was addicted to diet root beer. They also needed chewing gum and that would be for Sandy, who was using it as a placebo for her late, not so great smoking habit.

Olivia was surveying the chip selection—her own weakness was anything salty—when she heard someone enter the store through the back entrance where the truckers parked. Craning her neck, she glanced at the newcomer—male, big—dressed in a navy blue Seahawks jacket with a cap pulled very low on his face and an odd bouncing walk. Sunglasses, hands in pockets.

Her pulse picked up a notch. He looked familiar.

He went the other direction toward the beer case and she chided herself. Didn't the men at the front look familiar, too, and wasn't one of them a bigger than average guy? She was scatty, spooked from the events of the last three or four days. Large men were a mite scary right now, that was all.

The bell on the front door rang. She heard a woman's voice asking how to work a gas pump and the subsequent advice. Olivia chose a bag of BBQ chips and another of tortilla chips and started to put them in the basket.

She didn't even get her body turned before someone slammed into her from behind. "Sorry, lady," a male voice mumbled, but then clutching her with gloved hands, pinned her arms to her sides. When she struggled, he pressed her between the chip display and his hulking body, crushing the bags she still gripped. He pushed and released, pushed harder, didn't release, mashing her, subduing her. She couldn't even turn her head. He whispered in her ear. "Don't turn around. Don't say a word. You understand?"

Was it Grant? Hugh? One of the gamblers? A stranger? She couldn't tell, his voice was jerky, erratic, plus her own heartbeat roared in her ears. The coiled energy of his body seemed to shoot into her bones.

"Understand?" he repeated.

"Yes," she said, catching her breath. "Yes."

"You've been talking to that cop."

"Zac's a friend—"

"Shut up," he said pressing her so far into the display the wire rack bit into her cut cheek. She knew the store had huge convex mirrors installed for the clerks to keep an eye on remote corners. Were the men at the front just not paying attention, were they so caught up in the woman's gas pump travails they weren't looking? "You have something I want," he said.

"I don't…I…I don't know what it is. I don't know what you're looking for. Tell me…"

"Don't give me that. You were his partner, you know his secrets."

"No…"

"And give me all of it, too, or else. This is your last chance. Next time I'll come into your house. A bullet went through your husband like a hot poker through a snow ball. Imagine how fast it'll go through one of your kids."

Every drop of moisture in her mouth evaporated in a heartbeat. "I just need a little time," she mumbled against the rack. "You gave me twenty-four hours."

"I changed my mind. I can change it again."

"I—"

"Stay right here and count to one hundred. Slow. I might not shoot you, it might be that tin badge out front or one of the guys behind the counter. Do you want their blood on your hands?"

He unpinned her arms and moved away. The back door opened and closed with a chime. She was able to breathe again, but she didn't dare move, she counted as she'd been told to do, afraid if she didn't follow orders some innocent person would die. She was at ninety when a hand landed on her shoulder and she spun around, ready to come out fighting.

It was the bigger of the two clerks from behind the counter. He caught her fist on a downswing.

"Hey! What do you think you're doing?"

She swallowed a scream. "Did you see that man in the Seahawk's jacket?"

"Yeah, he went out the back door. Don't tell me he was shoplifting. I knew he was acting suspicious—"

She rushed to the back door and peered through the glass at the six or seven huge trucks pulled into the gas pumps.

The clerk followed her. "Hey, aren't you Olivia Capri, the lady who just had the four babies and your husband got shot—"

She turned panicked eyes his direction. "There's a cop out front. Get him in here. Hurry."

"But—"

"Just hurry!"

Chapter Seven

Olivia didn't wait around for Dilly to start questioning the truckers. All she could think of was getting home. As soon as she'd told Dilly what he wanted to know, she got in her car and sped off.

The back door was unlocked, the house deathly quiet. Running through the kitchen, she erupted into the living room, so caught up in anxiety that she didn't even think about the stress the quick, jerky movements made on her body.

The living room was empty. "Mother!" she yelled as she bolted into the nursery.

Her mother lay collapsed in one of the big rocking chairs, her mouth open, her arms flailed to her sides, her eyes closed. Olivia gasped. At the sound, Juliet Hart jerked awake with a gasp of her own.

And as one, all four babies started crying.

"What's wrong now?" her mother said, popping

to her feet, her hand atop her heart as though to keep it inside her chest. "Olivia?"

"Are you okay? Is everyone okay? Where are Tabitha and Sandy and Megan?"

"I think Sandy is asleep in your office and Tabitha is doing homework down in the basement. I think Megan is watching TV. What's wrong?"

This conversation was held in very loud voices in order to be heard over the incredible racket four tiny babies could create when sufficiently motivated. "I just got them down," Olivia's mother groaned, sliding Olivia a reproachable glance. "It took me forever to get Jillian asleep."

Olivia didn't care. She went from bassinet to bassinet, checking to see each with her own eyes, unshed tears blurring their dear, irate little faces. She picked up the last child, who happened to be Jillian, and held her close, kissing her sweet head over and over.

Tabitha looked in the door. "What's all the commotion about? Oh, hey, Olivia, did you get diet root beer?"

"Not exactly."

Tabitha rolled her eyes. At eighteen, she was the youngest of the Hart girls. All this baby watching had to be a real pain.

As Tabitha wandered off, Olivia's mom guided

Olivia to the rocker she'd just vacated. "Sit down. Tell me what happened."

Olivia sat, still holding Jillian. "Mom, I need to hold all my babies, all at the same time. Will you help me?"

One by one, her mother picked up the infants and brought them to Olivia along with a pillow or two for support. With the last child delivered, Olivia's arms and lap were full of babies who amazingly enough had all stopped crying and lay there gazing around the room as though taking inventory.

It felt wonderful to be safe in that small room with her children.

"Good thing I insisted on upholstered rockers," her mother said smugly. It was, too, because the children overflowed Olivia's lap. Once again she said, "Tell me what happened just now."

"Just give me a few minutes to catch my breath," Olivia said.

Juliet hitched her hands on her hips. "You look beat. Your poor face. How about a glass of juice?"

"I didn't actually buy juice," Olivia said.

"Milk?"

"I didn't get that, either. I didn't get anything."

This declaration was met with pursed lips, then "Well, how about a hot cup of tea? I think you still have tea, but we're going to have to send someone out shopping, we need that cereal for the babies' formula and we don't want Sandy to start smoking again."

"I know, Mom."

"You call me if you need me."

"Yes, and will you please go around to all the doors and windows and lock them?"

Her mother's eyebrows inched up her forehead, but she left the room. Olivia gazed down at the faces who stared up at her. They all had slate eyes, straight black hair, beautiful little noses and mouths. Each was a miniature work of art and it struck Olivia that though she wasn't sure what all these big men were looking for, Anthony had left an irreplaceable treasure in this house: four tiny children. Her children.

But the babies weren't what someone was willing to kill to get. As she stroked satin cheeks and silky hair, talking to the girls in a soft voice, she thought about getting an appraiser to come to the house and look at the things in Anthony's boxes. For that matter, she wasn't sure the intruder last night hadn't found what he came looking for but then if he had, why would he have cornered her in the store?

Unless it was a different man.

Her gaze fell on Anthony's mother's figurines atop the armoire, and she made a note to remember to check them over, too.

ZAC KNOCKED on the kitchen door. It was opened by Juliet Hart, who had just poured hot water into a mug from which a tea bag was suspended. He was glad to see her refasten the dead bolt behind him.

"I arranged for an alarm company to install alarms on all the doors and windows," he said. "They'll be here in an hour or so. I also talked to the landlord and he's going to give Olivia a break on the rent since she's adding improvements."

"Good," Juliet said. "Jack Porter came by earlier and fixed the basement door. Do you know why Olivia raced into the house like it was on fire?"

"Yeah." He told her about the incident at the convenience store as she leaned against the counter and listened.

"No wonder she acted so odd and wanted to know where everyone was. How about your sister?"

"I just talked to Faith and warned her to be careful. After she runs a quick errand for Dad she plans to come over here in case she can be some help."

"You take Olivia her tea and I'll go down and double-check the basement."

"I know Olivia is taking the kids to your place later today. Does your house have good security?"

"We have locks. Plus I have Olivia's father's old gun and I know how to use it."

"I'll send a deputy over, too," Zac said. He picked

up the mug and carried it through the house, pausing at the nursery door.

Olivia sat in the rocker, looking down at her brood, who occupied every square inch of her lap. What a picture she made—they all made. Olivia was dressed in a white shirt, her glossy black hair loose on her shoulders; her babies wore diapers and white T-shirts, their wispy black hair fluttering as she gently rocked the chair. Her hands wrapped around little legs and arms while tiny faces gazed up at her. With her head down, her hair fell over the bandage. She looked like a bountiful Madonna.

He'd seen a camera in the living room and softly withdrew to get it. At the sound of the electronic beeps, Olivia looked up startled, but then smiled. He'd caught one picture with her unaware he'd been there.

What would happen if he told her he loved her?

Just marched right in and said it?

He took a step.

"Did Dilly tell you about that man at the store?" she asked, her dark eyes frightened.

Professing love was premature at this point. He had to bide his time, he had to get her through this. He said, "Yeah, he did. He didn't find anyone matching your description out in the truck lot and no one out there admitted to seeing a damn thing. He also viewed the surveillance tape—impossible to tell much about the guy, except his general description fits everyone else you've seen."

"It has to be the guy from yesterday, one of the gamblers. Oh, Zac, I hate to say this, but I'm scared. Not for me, so much, as for everyone else, especially these little guys."

"I know you are."

"I'm going to reschedule Brianna's doctor's appointment and if the alarm gets installed here in time, I'm not going to take the babies out of this house. They're as safe here as anywhere else. And I'm going to also call an appraiser. There's one who works for the jewelry store where I used to do the books. I know the guy and trust him. I think I can persuade him to come here and look at Anthony's stuff."

It was a pleasure watching her revert to the old Olivia. She'd been under attack and frightened for so long he'd thought perhaps she'd never come back into her own in the same fierce temperamental way he knew and enjoyed. Of course, a small part of him worried this reinvigorated Olivia might not need him, but he didn't want her to need him so much as he wanted her to want him.

"One thing," he said. "If whatever Anthony was fencing is stolen, and let's be real, what are the chances it's not, then it's legally not yours to bargain with—"

"I know. But everyone thinks I was Anthony's partner in whatever he took or had or call it what you will. There's no way to convince them I'm not a party to it except to identify it and make a big deal out of giving it back. I was wondering if the Seattle cops could figure out what Anthony fenced—"

"They've got cops running around to known fences with Anthony's photo, but if it's ill-gotten goods, it's highly unlikely anyone will admit anything."

"If you catch the gamblers tonight—"

"Olivia, do you think the man in the convenience store was the bigger of that trio?"

"I don't know. It could have been. Did you hear back from Seattle? Was your partner able to ID them?"

"I haven't heard."

"It couldn't have been Grant, right?"

"It doesn't seem like his style."

"Anyway, he was with you."

"No, he wasn't."

"Yes, he came into the station as Roger Dilly and I were leaving. He was determined to talk to you."

"He didn't come into my office. I was on the phone. Hoopes was faxing the drawings to Seattle, but someone must have seen Grant if he came back there. The place is just a glorified hole in the wall."

"He couldn't have gotten all the way out to the highway, he didn't have time."

"Did you see him arrive? Did you see his red truck?"

"No—"

"So it's possible Hugh drove him over in the town car, it's possible Grant called Hugh as soon as he got inside and Hugh followed you out to the highway."

"Wait a second. Why would Hugh or Grant care about intimidating me? How would they know the gamblers had been at the house—"

"Everyone in Westerly knows everything about everybody," Zac said.

"True. Still. Maybe, maybe they killed Anthony, but using strong-arm tactics on me? Threatening infants? I can't quite believe that."

He put the cooling tea mug, which he just realized he was still holding, down on top of a dresser and crossed the room to perch on the edge of the other rocker. "Yeah, you're right. That's the trouble, there's just too much going on. The original break-in of your house with the blood spatters, Anthony's murder, the gamblers showing up, the basement intruder and sabotaged electricity and now this thing at the store. Add to that the fact that Anthony Capri is a giant question mark. I'm going to talk to my old partner about him, plus touch base on the gamblers' sketches we faxed this morning."

"It's a three-ring circus," Olivia said.

"Yeah, it is." He stared at the baby farthest down on Olivia's lap and said, "That baby has an orange toenail."

"Mango, actually," Olivia murmured with a loving look at her children. "That's how I know this baby is Antoinette." One by one, she touched three more tiny feet. "Jillian's toe is watermelon, Juliet's is lemon and Brianna's big toe is painted lime green." She moved a little and crooned, "What's the matter, Antoinette, are you slipping away?" When she tried to juggle the children back into position, a couple of them fussed.

He got up off the chair and took the one she'd called Antoinette, a five-pound charmer, but then they all were, and helped Olivia straighten the rest of them. Antoinette yawned and made a face and he smiled. What the hell, he kissed her forehead. It was the softest thing he'd ever touched.

Except maybe for her mother's lips.

The baby yawned again and scrunched knees and arms.

"I think she's tired."

"I woke them all up when I got home," Olivia said.

As Zac put Antoinette in the bassinet labeled with her name and a splotch of mango colored nail polish, the phone rang in the other room followed by a knock on the door. He was aware of new voices, mostly female, as he helped Olivia settle the other babies.

"The ladies from the hardware store are here for their turn with diaper changes and feedings. Zac, Deputy Hoopes is here, too, plus I saw the alarm installation van drive up," Olivia's mother called.

Olivia glanced at her watch. "The women from the hardware store are an hour early."

"I'll go see what Hoopes wants, then get the alarm guys working."

He walked into the living room to find it crowded with people. The three hardware employees were seated on the couch while his deputy stood by the door. One look at Hoopes's face and posture and Zac knew something was wrong.

Before he could ask, Olivia's sister, Sandy, erupted from the stairs leading up to the turret room. Her face was white and her lips quivered. With stricken eyes she looked from Olivia to Zac to Hoopes and stopped dead in her tracks.

"Zac—" Hoopes, said, and stopped.

"That was the hospital on the phone," Sandy said into the sudden silence. "It's Faith. She's been hurt."

A collective gasp filled the room, but it was Olivia's shocked sob that got through to Zac. He turned to encircle her with his arm.

"How bad is it?" Zac demanded.

"Pretty bad," Hoopes said. "It happened right outside your father's house. I didn't want you to hear about it on the phone. Detective Dilly said you aren't to worry about the office, he'll take care of things."

Olivia pushed Zac away. "You have to go."

"I have to go," he repeated woodenly. "But you—"

"What are you waiting for?"

Sandy's hands fluttered. "I'll stay here with Mom and the babies. You go too, Olivia."

"Call us when you find out how she is," her mother added.

Zac turned to Hoopes. "I want you plastered to this door. Don't let in anyone you don't know. When the alarm people are done here, I want you or someone else in the department in an unmarked vehicle across the street keeping surveillance on the house until further notice. I'll call Dilly. He'll arrange something."

The alarm installation crew showed up on the porch as Zac and Olivia raced past them to his squad car.

"Start with the basement," Zac called to them as he opened a door for Olivia.

AFTER A SEVEN-MINUTE drive with the siren screeching and Zac amazingly holding a conversation on the phone with Dilly, they arrived at the hospital to find Faith still in the E.R. Zac's dad was standing by the glass doors wearing jeans and an old gray sweater, slippers on his feet. Olivia put her arms around him and felt his shoulders heave.

"It's pretty bad," Gus Bishop said, his voice thin.

Zac put his arms around both of them.

After a few moments they pulled apart, but Olivia kept hold of Gus' hand. She knew how much his children meant to him, especially Faith, the baby of the family, the glue since Mrs. Bishop died twenty years before.

"How is she?" Olivia asked.

Gus shook his head. "She was covered with blood. At first I thought she was dead." He seemed to really see Olivia for the first time and he choked out, "You, too, honey? What happened to you?"

"Nothing important. I'm fine."

"Dad, what happened?" Zac asked. His gaze was darting around and Olivia thought he was probably looking for a nurse, but they were ominously absent.

"Faith was getting out of her car. She'd parked it out on the street like she always does, you know, out in front of my place. Then the lady across the street said she saw another car turn the corner and head right for her. It hit her and then took off like a bat out of hell. I heard an engine gun and some tires squealing so I went outside and there she was…she was—"

His voice caught and he looked up at his tall, broad-shouldered son. "Who would do something like this to my little girl? What kind of person does something like this?"

"I don't know, Dad. Did the witness get a license number or a car model or anything?"

"Not much of anything. It was the widow Farley who saw all this. She said it was a dark car, big, but she wasn't wearing her glasses, so who knows. Who would want to hurt Faith? Sweetest girl in the world. And it's my fault. If I hadn't asked her to drop by with the damn newspaper, she wouldn't be laying in there."

Gus squeezed Olivia's hand and withdrew a few paces, wiping his eyes with a tissue.

Overcome with remorse and guilt, Olivia moved away to peer through the glass doors, trying in vain to see past the curtains and knot of doctors and nurses.

Zac came up behind her and put his arm around her. She leaned her head against his shoulder. "It's my fault she's in there," she said.

"Stop that," he said. "It's not your fault and it's not Dad's fault. Whoever was driving that car—"

"You know it has to be connected to these threats. I was worried about Faith and my mother and sisters and even you, but mostly I was worried about my babies. I never dreamed—"

"Hush," he said, wrapping his arms around her. "Your twenty-four-hour deadline isn't over yet."

"It doesn't matter. That man in the convenience store said he could change his mind again. He's making a point of scaring me but why didn't he run me down instead of Faith?"

"Honey—"

"You need to take care of your sister and your dad. I'm fine. Tell me what I can do to help."

He smiled at her and as his lips curved, she remembered kissing him the night before. So much had happened since, then it had driven the memory away for a while, but it came back now with a jolt. She pushed it aside to examine later and added, "I want to help."

"Go sit with Dad, keep him talking. I'm going to go see what I can find out. I'll be right back."

"She has to be okay, Zac. She just has to be."

"I know," he said, stroking her face, peering into her eyes. "I know."

OLIVIA ACCEPTED a ride home from Deputy Kellerman, a man she hadn't met yet as he'd just graduated from the police academy and been hired in Westerly while she was away. He was fresh-faced and very serious.

As much as she hated leaving Zac and Gus, she'd been told she'd have to wait to see Faith until morning. The unspoken questions were, would Faith live through the night, would she survive the surgery to remove her spleen and set her bones, would she regain consciousness?

Zac had insisted she go back to her babies, promising to call the minute anything happened, good or bad. Olivia had no idea how any of them were supposed to get through the next twelve hours, but she did agree that her place was with her babies.

She climbed the steps slowly. Pain and fatigue were constant companions now, the quiet rest the doctor had encouraged nothing but a pipe dream. So much had happened in so little time she could barely think straight. She'd been home a little over twenty-four hours.

The house sported a state-of-the-art alarm system and after checking on the babies who were receiving the tail end of a feeding by a bunch of Tabitha's friends, she spent a while learning how to work it. She kept glancing at the clock. Surely the gamblers wouldn't come back tonight, not after the incident at the store, but it was hard not to react to every small noise.

She called the appraiser who said he would come by the next morning and though it was on the tip of her tongue to beg him to come that night, she knew there was work that needed to be done beforehand. She had yet to go down to the basement and see what the midnight intruder had possibly taken and investigate the figurines…

Who knew what tragedy might await the morning? What if Faith didn't make it? The list of her injuries was terrifying. Olivia caught herself tearing up and shook her head. No more crying. She would remain hopeful and positive if it killed her.

The new deputy took over for Hoopes when they got back to the house. She peeked out the front window, comforted by the white van across the street. She busied herself doing a load of laundry while her mother and sisters took a break.

Within an hour, the babies would start waking up again for another feeding. It was a never-ending process with four of them, starting again almost as soon as it stopped. Olivia still attempted to nurse them on a rotating schedule and would as long as she could.

When she delivered a basket of clean spit-up rags back to their room, she paused for a moment by the armoire. Reaching up, she grabbed the nearest figurine Anthony's mother had left him, a bowing woman wearing a flowing blue dress, holding a fan, the toe of one shoe peeking out from under her gown as she looked down smiling, presumably at a kneeling suitor. Olivia turned it over and found a small pink stamp on the bottom, illegible, and a hole. She stuck her finger in the hole and wiggled it around. No diamonds or drugs or anything else emerged.

She looked at the painted porcelain face. Ruby-red lips, golden hair, blue eyes, blushed cheeks. She looked like Faith.

Olivia put the figurine back atop the armoire where it seemed to smile down at her along with the other four. Enough for each girl to have one someday, a tiny piece of their father's history. All of them were much the same, women dressed for a ball, some wearing tiaras, some with raised arms, all slightly different.

There was also a plaster bell that Anthony's mother had made in a pottery class, an ungainly mess of a project. Olivia picked it up next. It was about eight inches high and six inches in diameter, painted a muted silver with obvious plastic baubles sunk into the finish. The clapper looked like a painted fishing lure dangling from twine, the inside was signed in a bold *M* standing for Mom, Olivia thought, or maybe a first name like Mary. Careful not to jingle it, Olivia put it back where she'd found it, wondering how long sentiment demand she keep the thing.

Sighing, she picked up the laundry basket. If she

hurried she'd have time to go downstairs and investigate the boxes again, too.

There was a faint knock on the front door. Olivia glanced at her watch. It was after eight, almost dark, almost the same time of day as yesterday when the gamblers came. She froze a second as the knocks grew louder. Whoever it was would wake the babies if they persisted and almost anything was better than that.

As she approached the door, she peered out the front window. Deputy Kellerman strode purposely across her lawn, on his way to the stoop, hand on his gun in its holster. A small white compact was parked at the curb. She waited until she heard Kellerman's voice and an answering remark, then carefully opened the door.

A tall man in his early forties turned from talking to the deputy. "Mrs. Capri?" he said in a pleasant, easy voice as his gaze shifted away from the bandage on her cheek.

"Do I know you?" she asked.

"My name is Brad Makko."

He said it in such a way that Olivia got the impression it was supposed to mean something to her. She met Kellerman's curious gaze and shrugged.

On the other hand, Brad Makko did look familiar. The way he held his body, for instance. He had blondish hair, dark blue eyes, and thin lips topped with a very tidy mustache. He was dressed casually but his jeans and Western-style shirt reeked high quality and his boots looked like alligator.

"I don't believe we've met," Olivia said.

"No, of course not. I had rather hoped my brother might have mentioned me, though. He and I were estranged but I had hopes of patching things up with him someday."

"Your brother?"

"Your husband, Mrs. Capri. I'm your husband's brother, Brad."

"But you can't be. My husband's family is all dead."

"No," Brad Makko said calmly. "As a matter of fact, that's not true. There are things you need to know that only I can tell you. Will you talk to me?"

Olivia's heart sank. *What now…?*

Chapter Eight

"Your last names aren't the same," she said.

"There's a lot you probably don't know about… your husband. If we could talk for a while, maybe inside?"

"I'm not sure," Olivia said, glancing at Kellerman again.

The deputy said, "There's been some trouble here lately, sir. You mind showing me some ID?"

Brad slipped a wallet out of his inside jacket pocket. "Of course not."

"It says he's Brad Makko from Las Vegas, Nevada, all right," Kellerman said, holding a small flashlight on the driver's license, then flashing it up to check it against the man standing in front of him. Narrowing suspicious eyes, he added, "You mind if I call it in?"

"Absolutely not," Brad said quickly. "I know my brother was murdered, I've been keeping up with the investigation in the news. From the looks of things, you still haven't caught the fiend who killed him?"

"I'm not at liberty to talk about the investigation," Kellerman said. "Please stay outside until I check this out."

"I hope you're not offended by all this," Olivia said, as Kellerman trotted off. She felt awkward and decided the situation demanded a little humility on her part. If this really was Anthony's brother, it probably wasn't the welcome he'd anticipated but too many odd things had happened lately to take anyone at face value.

Brad Makko reached into his jacket pocket again and brought out a half dozen pictures. "I brought along a few photos. Unfortunately, there aren't too many left, but, well, take a look." He handed the short stack to Olivia.

Some were color snapshots, obviously old, others were on card stock like from a photographer's studio. The first two were of two small blond boys. One included a plump woman filling a wading pool as they danced around her in bathing trunks, the other showed the same boys a year or so later standing on a sidewalk in front of a tract house.

"That's our mother with us when my brother and I were three and five years old respectively. That other one Mom took on my brother's first day of kindergarten."

Olivia studied the smallest of the boy's faces. Would her daughters resemble their father as they grew? Their coloring was so different, it was hard to tell. Maybe in the eyes…

The next photo showed Anthony at eighteen or so. His smile leaped off the paper and Olivia felt her gut twist.

"His graduation from high school," Brad said.

Olivia shuffled down another layer and Brad chuckled. "That's him at a party, wearing a lamp-shade and a toga. He went to Harvard, you know."

"Yes. He was very proud of that."

"He got a scholarship. I know it was hard on him not fitting in with the wealthier kids. I think that's why he never finished."

"What do you mean? He graduated."

"He told you that?"

"Yes. Well, actually, I have a friend who's in law enforcement. He started a background research on Anthony before I married him, but I told my friend to stop being so suspicious." She paused, wishing now she'd not stopped Zac from finding out every-thing he could about Anthony.

You wouldn't have your babies. Already it was impossible to imagine life without them.

Now she said, "Are you telling me the records were wrong?"

"We'll talk about that in a few minutes, okay?"

She revealed the last picture, this one relatively recent. It showed Anthony and Brad with their arms around one another's shoulders, squinting into the sun, smiling as they had when they were boys.

"My wife took that one when my brother stopped and visited us on his way up here from his home in Texas."

"Anthony never lived in Texas—"

"He didn't tell you, huh? Olivia, we need to talk."

Olivia heard noises inside the house, including the unmistakable cry of a small baby. As usual, her body responded in an automatic physiological manner. "Would you please sit on the bench over there? Let the deputy do his job and check you out while I go inside and get a sweater. I'll be back in a moment."

"That's just fine," Brad said, and proceeded to take a seat on the bench running along the front of the porch. "I know you just had quadruplets and may I say you look remarkable, especially for a woman who's been through what you have. I can't wait to meet my nieces, but all in good time."

Olivia went back inside and locked the door behind her. She could hear her mother and Tabitha in with the babies and she ducked her head into the room. "Can you handle things for a while? You'll never guess who just showed up at the front door."

"The gamblers!" Juliet gasped, joggling her namesake whose whimpering changed to a howl.

"Careful there, Mom." She took the baby and rocked her in her arms for a few seconds until she quieted down into the hiccups which she'd have to get over before they tried to feed her. "It's Anthony's brother, a guy named Brad Makko," Olivia said in a singsong voice Juliet seemed to respond to.

"Anthony didn't have any family—"

"Well, it looks as though he had a brother. I'm going to go talk to him out on the porch if you can spare me for this feeding."

"Sure. Tabitha, go wake up Megan. The three of us should be fine. The gals from the Bowl-a-Rama league are coming later tonight to help out." Turning back to Olivia, she added, "Did you hear anything from Zac? I wonder if Faith is out of surgery yet."

"He hasn't called. I'll take my phone outside with me and tell you if I hear from him."

Her mother sat in a rocker and held out her arms. "Let me have my little angel, I'll get her settled."

Olivia reluctantly returned her first-born to her mother and grabbed her sweater. She went outside just as Deputy Kellerman returned from his car. "It all checks out," he said, handing Brad Makko his wallet. "Thank you for being so cooperative."

"No problem," Brad said.

Olivia sat down on the edge of the planter across from him as the deputy walked back across the yard.

"I hope you don't mind talking outside, Mr. Makko. My family is feeding my babies. There would no privacy inside."

"Please, call me Brad." He studied her face again, and this time his gaze lingered on her injuries. "Were you hurt because of my brother's death?"

"Indirectly," she said.

"I'm real sorry to hear that. No, I don't blame you for being cautious, Olivia. In fact, I applaud it. Have to admit, however, it would sure mean a lot to me if I could see those little girls with my own eyes. There was just the briefest of glimpses on the television a few days ago. They're my nieces, you know, the only ones I have, the only ones I'll ever have now. I just can't believe Danny is dead."

"Danny?"

"Your husband's real name is—was—Danny Makko, not Anthony Capri."

Olivia took a deep breath. "I don't know if I even want to hear this," she said. "He told me so many lies."

"Yeah, well that was Danny's way."

A light went on in Olivia's head. "That's why there was a discrepancy about what happened in college. Zac, my friend, investigated a man named Anthony Capri."

"Listen, Olivia, at that press conference when your mother held up the photo of someone named Anthony Capri and I recognized my little brother, I don't mind telling you I was damn surprised."

If she hadn't given birth to quadruplets, Anthony's and her story wouldn't have made the news and if her mother hadn't held up a picture of Anthony, this man wouldn't have connected the name to his brother, he might never have known about his nieces or the fact his brother was dead.

"Let me get this straight. My husband's real name was Danny Makko. You're his brother and obviously not as dead as Anthony—as Danny—reported. What about your parents?"

"Dad disappeared when Danny and I were little kids, the summer that picture with our mother was taken, as a matter of fact. Mom is suffering premature Alzheimer's now. She's in a home and doesn't know me from a hole in the ground."

"But she's alive."

"Yes."

"I have several figurines my husband said she bequeathed him."

"Figurines?"

"Old-fashioned women in gowns. Porcelain."

"Oh, mother's dolls. I wondered where they'd gone. I'm delighted you have them."

"But your mother isn't dead."

He smiled sadly. "That's true. Maybe I should take them to her."

Olivia smiled. "If she's really suffering from extreme dementia, will it matter? I just mean that they're all I have of my babies' father to pass on to them."

"I see," Brad said. "Well, of course, you must keep them, then."

"I have his Super Bowl ring in my safe. You can have that—"

"He bought that at a pawn shop when he was in Vegas. Did he tell you he drove NASCAR, too?"

She sighed heavily. "He wasn't a pilot or a deep-sea diver—"

"No. He was a con man, pure and simple. To his credit, he was a damn good con man, but that's all." Resting his elbows on his knees, he folded his hands and stared at his laced fingers as he continued. "I'm going to be perfectly honest with you, Olivia. You deserve the truth. I've been picking up after my little brother most of his life. He was an habitual liar, moving through identities the way some people move through careers. In and out of trouble. Served a couple of years in prison for fraud. But two years ago when he came through Vegas, he swore he was finished with all that and I believed him. He had a knack for saying whatever you needed to hear."

"I know," Olivia said, amazed at how detached

she felt from Anthony in a little under a week. It was like peeling away layers of an onion until there was absolutely nothing left. It stunned her that she'd been so taken in, and yet here was a man who had known Anthony—Danny—since birth and had still allowed himself to be led down the garden path.

"Maybe we see and hear what we want to see and hear," she added.

"Maybe we do."

"So, after he left Vegas, then what happened?"

"He called a time or two and then we got a visit from a gal who claimed she knew Danny really well and was trying to find him. She'd traced him as far as our place."

"Who was she?"

He looked Olivia in the eye, took a deep breath and said, "Danny's wife."

The words hung there between them. Olivia was just plain speechless.

"She had documents, you know, a marriage certificate and photographs…"

Olivia held up a hand to still him. Her heart beat like a hummingbird's wings. She finally said, "Did you call your brother?"

"Damn sure I did. He told me some elaborate story about her being a stalker and when I refused to believe him, he told me he'd take care of it. His wife tried to trace him—he'd cleaned out her bank account when he left her and stolen from a lot of investors who were under the impression he was a cattle rancher. She wanted her money back. Anyway, she contacted me later and told me the private eye she'd hired couldn't find him, said it was as though he'd disappeared into thin air."

"Did she divorce him?" Olivia asked.

"No."

"So she's still married to him, or was until someone killed him."

His mouth moved as though he was tasting the words before he finally spit them out. "Yes, I'm afraid so. He was still married to a woman named Lindy."

"So I was never really married to your brother?"

"No."

A short giggle bubbled from her lips.

"Olivia?"

She waved away his concern, tried to assume a properly outraged expression, but laughter churned inside, seeking an outlet.

"I am sure this distresses you to no end—"

It was no use trying to contain it, easier perhaps to recork a bottle of champagne. The craziness of the situation gurgled up her throat and she just couldn't help it, she laughed out loud and with gusto, and seeing Brad Makko's stunned response just made her laugh louder. Tears filled her eyes and rolled down her cheeks, but these tears were different, these tears were more about relief than sadness.

The door flew open to reveal Olivia's mother and sister each holding a baby, staring openmouthed at her. Olivia tried to control herself, but their shocked expressions started a new attack of the giggles. She was aware Deputy Kellerman trotted across the grass again, gun drawn this time and she laughed even harder. All that was missing were three gamblers, the Robinson brothers and a hulk in a Seahawks jacket.

The laughter stopped as abruptly as it had begun when Faith's image filled her head. Faith hit so hard she flew into in the air, landing in a broken heap. Faith lying on the road, battered, bloody, near death, her father running to her side.

Covering her mouth with her hand, Olivia got to her feet and ran past her startled family into the house, barely making it to the bathroom in time.

A SHARP, COLD WIND had come up during that interminable day spent sitting in the hospital while Faith fought for her life. She was out of surgery now. Zac's father was in the ICU with her, refusing to leave.

Zac hated running out on his dad, but the truth was he needed some sleep if he was going to be able to function the next day. He also wanted to touch base with Olivia.

That's all it was, just his need to tell Olivia that Faith had survived the surgery, his need to see her face when she heard the news, to share her relief. If Faith was out of the woods in the morning, he had to drive to Seattle, he had to attend that trial, he wanted to meet with Dave and he wanted to see Olivia first.

The house was brightly lit for after nine o'clock, but he imagined time on a clock face held little meaning for the four petal-soft despots who kept their own schedules. He smiled when he thought of the one he'd held that morning. He had to think for a second to remember her name. Antoinette. That was it. He'd never thought of himself as a baby man, but there was something about these four that touched him deeply.

Maybe it was their mother, maybe it was knowing their father was dead, maybe he was just plain getting soft.

He pulled up behind a squad car parked across the street. Kellerman got out to meet him and the two of them stood in the middle of the empty street for a moment, staring at the house.

"She's got a visitor," Kellerman said.

"What do you mean a visitor? Half the town is going in and out of there all day and night."

"The vic's brother."

"The vic's—you mean Anthony Capri? He didn't have any family—"

"Well, this guy claims he's the brother. I checked him out. Name is Brad Makko from Las Vegas, Nevada. Forty-two, married—"

"What do you mean you checked him out?" Zac interrupted.

"I mean I ran his license and he is who he says he is."

"That doesn't make him related to Anthony."

Kellerman stared at the house for a second. "But he had pictures and—"

"Where is he now?"

"Inside the house."

Zac turned quickly, the knot in his gut tightening with each long stride. He tried the knob and the door opened which kind of negated the effectiveness of the alarm system and he swore under his breath.

Olivia sat on the sofa next to man who must be Brad Makko. Her eye had assumed full discoloration and the bandage on her cheek looked as worn out as he felt. The rest of her family milled about the room, most with a baby in arms. As soon as he appeared, every face turned to him and Olivia stood abruptly, expression fearful. "Is Faith—is she—"

"She made it through surgery," he said, his gaze never straying far from Makko, who bore a certain surface resemblance to Anthony. The coloring was similar, the eyes. He looked about the same size, too, though twenty pounds lighter. Sticking out a hand, Zac said, "I don't believe we've met."

Makko stood up and shook Zac's hand. "You must be Olivia's friend. I was so sorry to hear about your sister's accident."

Zac nodded, straining not to grit his teeth. What happened to Faith was no accident, not by any stretch of the imagination. He turned his attention back to Olivia and said, "The doctors are cautiously optimistic. She still hasn't regained consciousness."

"How is your dad?"

"Still with her. May we talk, Olivia?"

"Of course," she said.

"Let's go in the kitchen. I could use a drink of water."

"Sure." She turned to Makko. "I'll be a moment."

"I'll mosey back to the hotel and see you tomorrow."

"I was hoping you'd have the opportunity to look over a few of your brother's things with me. And you wanted to see your mother's figurines—"

"To tell you the truth, I'm kind of tired. Drove all the way from Roseberg, Oregon, today. How about I come back in the morning? I'd love to see the babies one more time before I head south. The wife will kill me if I don't take a few pictures."

"If that's what you want, that's fine."

"Olivia?" Zac said.

Brad Makko said good-bye. Zac made a big deal out of locking the door and arming the alarm system once he was gone, then he went into the kitchen where he found Olivia putting ice cubes in a tall glass and filling it with water. The room was heavily shadowed as the only lights came from appliances and an under the counter unit.

For a few seconds he feasted on the sight of her glossy black hair laying on her shoulders and the succulent way her curves filled out the back of her jeans. She'd always been a runner with slim hips, but for the moment, she appeared rounder, softer. He liked her both ways.

"I know what you're going to say," she said as she turned, averting her gaze. Had she felt him devouring her with his eyes? He reined in his imagination and took the proffered glass. "You do?"

"Brad Makko was inside the house because I had a meltdown."

He almost spit an ice cube across the room. This is not what he'd expected her to say. "What do you mean? A meltdown?"

"He told me things about his brother. Terrible things."

"Well, you know Anthony—"

"Anthony wasn't really Anthony. His name was

Danny Makko. He did time in prison for fraud, he stole from people, he lied about being a sports hero and a pilot and everything else. Brad says he changed his identity several times, always after some kind of swindle."

"But I contacted Harvard—"

"With the wrong name. Anyway, that's not the worst of it."

"It gets worse?"

"Danny Makko had a wife named Lindy. She's his real widow, not me. I was never married to Anthony Capri. I was never even married to Danny Makko."

He set the glass down hard on the drain board. "There could be a world of former cohorts and victims who wanted to get even. Now instead of three or four suspects, we could have three or four dozen. I'll need to talk to Brad Makko before he leaves town and then share this with Seattle tomorrow. Plus, let's be cautious, let's check out Makko and determine if he really is who he says he is."

Zac pushed aside the possibility that tomorrow would hold horrors of a different kind, knowing if Faith got worse or didn't pull through, none of the rest of this would matter much, at least not for a while.

Except, of course, how it affected Olivia and her children.

With a deep breath, he added, "I assume hearing your supposed husband already had a wife is when you had your meltdown."

"Yep. I started laughing."

"Laughing? Not crying?"

"Nope, gut-busting laughter. I couldn't stop and then I thought about what had happened to Faith earlier today and how scared I was for her and my stomach flipped. It wasn't pretty." She moved a little closer and said, "I could use a hug."

He reached out and pulled her into his arms. Laying her head against his chest and circling his waist, she said, "Do the doctors really think Faith is going to be okay?"

"They're not making promises, but the surgery was successful and they said she was lucky. She's bandaged from head to toe, cut and bruised and un-conscious—she doesn't look lucky to me. Dad's with her in the ICU. He said he wouldn't sleep at home. All the nurses know him from his heart surgery last year, so they're spoiling him rotten."

She tilted her head and looked up at him. Her lips were just inches from his.

"While I was occupied, my mother invited Brad Makko into the house. By the time I got cleaned up, he'd shown her all the pictures he brought with him.

Mom and he were getting along like gangbusters and Deputy Kellerman was sitting on the chair holding a baby, so we all kind of relaxed."

"How did Makko know—"

"About the man we thought was Anthony? He caught the national news the night they picked up the interview from the hospital. He said when my mother held up his brother's picture he knew he had to come up here and tell me the truth. He says he's been cleaning up after his brother for years. And then the next day he heard about the murder."

"Describe the photos," he said, wishing they could stop talking. The fact she could so easily resist him when they were this close was, to say the least, discouraging. His body was on fire. He wanted her so much it was hard to form a coherent thought.

He listened as she told him about the photos. "Hmm," he said when she finished. "It sounds as though you have a new relative of sorts."

"Just what I need. Oh, he's a nice enough guy. I thought I'd get him to help me look through his brother's things tomorrow before the appraiser comes. He might know something about some of it. For instance, he told me his brother bought the Super Bowl ring at a pawn shop."

Zac resisted the very fierce urge to gloat. He'd known the guy was a phony from the start. If he hadn't been so worried jealousy was making him paranoid he wouldn't have listened when Olivia warned him to back off. As it was, he'd suspended the background search immediately.

"I'm going to let Kellerman go home. I'll stay here for the night on the couch. The man from the store is still running loose as are the three gamblers who came to your door. It worries me they've disappeared. People like that don't give up easily."

"Maybe the Seattle cops caught up with them."

"Maybe, I guess I'll find out tomorrow."

"Or maybe they were behind what happened to Faith."

"I called in a vacationing deputy to stand guard at the hospital tonight so she and dad are covered."

"Your department must be stretched pretty thin."

They both fell quiet. He kept expecting her to step out of his embrace, but she leaned into him instead. The ripe weight of her body was causing all sorts of reactions in his. He imagined if a miracle occurred and she demanded he make love to her right that moment, the whole thing would be over before it started. Some lover he'd make.

So, they'd just have to do it again. And again. For a lifetime, if need be. A man couldn't expect too much out of himself when the fire in his groin had been stoked this long.

"What are you thinking?" she said softly.

"You don't want to know."

"I was thinking about our kiss last night," she said.

He looked down and met her gaze. "You apologized for it. Why?"

A lovely smile curved her lips. She was all curves, from her hair to her breasts to her waist to her derrière to her calves to her ankles. He wanted to kiss and fondle every inch of her.

She said, "The kiss last night was better than the one when I was seventeen."

"Even though you were half-asleep?"

"I knew what was going on. I shouldn't have taken advantage of your kindness. That's why I apologized."

For a moment he froze. *Kindness?* Finally he mumbled, "Is that what you think I was doing, being…being kind?"

"Well, yes."

For some reason he couldn't identify, the word *kind* rubbed him every wrong way. It negated his feelings, it negated what he had kind of hoped was budding between them, what he'd sensed or wanted to sense maybe. The word confused and annoyed him.

She said, "I mean, why else?"

Stunned by how dense she could be, he repeated, "Why else?"

"Oh, come off it, Zac. I know you don't want to

hurt my feelings, but I'm not some nubile seven-teen-year-old anymore. I've just had four babies, my body shows wear and tear, I've made some terrible decisions that have hurt people we both care about. I cry at the drop of a hat or laugh when I shouldn't—"

"Oh, be quiet," he said.

She licked her lips, looked startled and said, "I was just trying to explain I understood your kindness—"

"Let me show you how kind I really am," he grumbled, and knowing he was about to blow caution out of the water with a howitzer, cupped her head in his hands and lowered his face until his lips crushed against hers. Kind? He'd show her kind. He'd ravage her if that's what it took.

He pried her lips apart with his tongue and claimed her mouth, rolling his tongue around hers, his hands tangled in her hair, then running up and down her body, over her breasts, pulling her closer against his arousal, in one instant afraid he was hurting her, in the next not caring. Surely, any moment now his passion would burn away their clothes and leave them stark naked in each others arms. Fine with him.

What would she do if he stripped her bare and lifted her up on the counter and came to her?

Kind? How dare she accuse him of a sympathy

kiss when it took every ounce of willpower he had just to keep from consuming her?

She pushed herself away from him, eyes glistening, fingers touching her lips as if to make sure she'd escaped with them intact. The next moment she was back against him, arms once again encircling him, face buried against his chest.

Sighing, he slowly closed his arms around her. "Olivia. Oh, God, I'm sorry."

"No, no it's not you, it's me. I mess up everything I touch."

They stood for several moments, him leaning back against the counter, her pressed against him. He was hoping her family didn't choose that moment to come into the kitchen. He closed his eyes as she finally resumed her soft murmurs, straining hard to catch her words as he could tell she was trying to say something.

"Everything is happening so fast I don't have time to think," she whispered. "A week ago I was a married woman and if you'd asked me if I loved my husband I would have said of course I do. Now I'm clinging to you when you have a murder investigation to conduct, Faith is in ICU and the demands of a new job are running you ragged. I'm putting a lot of pressure on you and your men and I don't know what to do about it because I'm so afraid. And because I'm so afraid, I don't trust my feelings." She stepped away at last and cast him an under-the-eyelash glance. "Do you understand what I'm saying?"

He nodded. Sort of. He'd known it was too soon to put demands on her, but there it was, it was out in the open now.

She wiped her face with shaky fingers, moving away to the paper-towel dispenser and tearing off a sheet. Regarding him from a safe distance, she added, "Maybe we're drawn together by circumstances, that's all. I mean, we've known each other forever, we've been friends, but we've never dated, we've never been romantic, we've both married other people. Well, you have, anyway. I just thought I did."

"And when this is over, you think we'll go back to that."

She nodded. "Right now you're in full rescue mode and I'm in full damsel-in-distress mode. I've been sending you all sorts of mixed signals."

"Olivia, damn it all." He stared at her for a moment then down at his boots, then back at her. "I'm in lo—"

"Don't say it," she interrupted, holding up a hand. "I couldn't bear it if you said it."

"Why?"

"Because it doesn't mean anything," she whispered.

"What are you talking about?"

"I've heard the words before," she said softly, "and they didn't mean a damn thing."

"You're comparing me to that bastard you married?"

She met his gaze and dropped it.

"The difference," he said, "is that your late, great, not-so-much a husband used those words to get what he wanted. They were a tool in his bag of tricks. And frankly, if you can't tell the difference between him and me, then you're the one in trouble."

He took a deep breath, regretting his outburst almost at once. Talk about kicking someone when they were down. "Let's just shelve all of this," he added. "I got carried away tonight, that's all."

The relief that flooded her face broke his heart into another million pieces. She whispered, "Okay."

At least he knew where he stood. She didn't love him. She didn't even trust the idea of love. It was time to walk away.

"Friends?" she added.

He wanted to tell her no, he couldn't be her friend. It had gone too far in him for that. But he couldn't do it to her, he couldn't compound her grief and guilt, he wasn't thinking clearly himself.

A baby's cry reached the kitchen. Olivia glanced at the door, panic on her face. She started blotting her eyes as though afraid the distress of the last few moments showed.

He said, "Take your time. Don't worry, your mom and sisters and I can handle things."

Without waiting for a response, he pushed his way into the living room, the connecting door swishing shut on his heels, the sound it made a lot like the prolonged sigh of a farewell.

Chapter Nine

In her dream, Zac was falling off a high cliff, calling her name, as behind her somewhere, louder by the second, a marching band grew closer, horns blaring, out of tune, increasingly shrill…

She awoke to a jarring combination of sounds that included the high-pitched beep of the fire alarm, the deeper register of the new alarm system and the cries of babies.

She stumbled out of her bedroom and into the hall where she found her mother and sisters gathering in the living room, looking as disorientated as she felt. Zac hurried through the nursery door carrying a baby in each arm.

"Here, everyone take a baby, make sure you grab a blanket. It's cool outside. Hurry, there's smoke coming through the kitchen door, go out the front way. Get far away from the house in case the fire reaches the oxygen tanks in the nursery. Hurry."

Megan and Tabitha each took a child from Zac

and made for the front door while Sandy and Olivia's mother dashed into the nursery to get the other two. Zac caught Olivia's arm.

"Get everyone way from the house. There are oxygen tanks in here and they could blow. I'm going after whoever triggered the intruder alarm."

He'd thrown on his jeans and nothing else. His bare chest glowed warmly in the twilit room. He looked muscular and capable, powerful, eyes flashing with determination. It gave her confidence just to look at him. He pulled on boots without socks and she realized her own feet were bare and she was dressed in a flimsy nightgown.

His gaze dropped down her body, his eyes so intense that when they flew back to her face she felt naked.

"Hurry," he repeated, grabbing his gun from the table.

He ran through the open front door and disappeared into the night. Olivia could hear approaching sirens from outside. She took Brianna from her mother and joined everyone else on the front lawn, counting heads, making sure all were safe.

She expected to see leaping flames climbing into the night sky, eating her roof, destroying what worldly possessions she had left, but all she saw was smoke billowing from the back. Zac was nowhere in sight. Neighbors wearing nightclothes started to arrive, and still carrying Brianna, Olivia searched the crowd for Zac. She heard her name and looked around. No one met her gaze, no one motioned at her. Maybe it came from around back. It was hard to tell with the baby's whimpers in her ear and all the other noise. It had to be Zac.

"Shh, baby. Shh, sweetheart," she crooned. "Let's go find Grandma."

As the fire trucks approached, she found her mother, sisters and other three children in a knot of neighbors who were suggesting the babies be brought inside the house across the street to keep warm. Olivia handed Brianna to her mother, kissing the child's downy forehead before she let go. "I have to find Zac. He called me."

"Take my sweater, dear," a neighbor said, handing Olivia a black sweater to shrug on over her gown.

Looking over Olivia's head at the house beyond, her mother said, "Oh, your poor house."

"It doesn't matter as long as all of us are safe. Watch the babies, Mom. I'll be right back." She kissed each child, a foot, a cheek, a tiny clenched fist, whatever was handy, before watching everyone traipse across the street.

The firemen were loosening hoses, yelling directions as she made her way around the side of the house. The alarms were as loud as ever.

Olivia saw Zac at the far edge of the property,

behind the garage, bending over, examining something on the ground. Coughing from the smell of the smoke, she wondered who or what was on the ground. She moved as fast as she could considering her bare feet and the rocks on the path.

The thought of facing Zac again was disquieting. What had happened between them had been a disaster and she'd allowed it to happen. She'd baited him by talking about their kiss and touching him whenever she had the opportunity and when he'd acted on it all, she'd rebuked him.

And then he'd closed down and returned the favor and she couldn't blame him a bit.

The other two times their lips had touched it had been gentle, kind of romantic, but not this time. This kiss had been a tornado and like a tornado, it had lifted both of them off their feet and deposited them a world away where the landscape was different, where the language wasn't the same.

A *Wizard of Oz* kiss.

She'd never been kissed like that before, with such need and abandon, with such desire. It had terrified her. No, that wasn't true. The kiss had been exhilarating, it had been her own personal response that scared her. The need she'd felt and not trusted, the desire she experienced that seemed so out of place, the hope…

And now the damn house was on fire.

Looking at the half-lit expanse of Zac's bare back and shoulders, flames of a different nature licked the inside of her thighs. She hugged herself against the midnight chill and picked up her pace, walking close by a hedge of rhododendrons to avoid the rocks. When she heard a rustle from within the bushes, she froze for a second, her heartbeat skittering around in her chest. Was someone in there or was it an animal, maybe one of the many dogs that lived on the street? It seemed unlikely an animal would lurk so close…

Behind the garage, Zac stood up, looking the other way, totally oblivious to her as she moved through the heavily shadowed yard wearing a dark sweater. For a second she just stared at him, and wished…wished so many things. That she was braver, that she hadn't made such terrible decisions, that she hadn't hurt him…

It finally dawned on her he wasn't looking around as though expecting her. In fact, he'd started walking briskly toward the front of the house, away from the shape on the ground, away from her. The house alarms finally stopped blaring.

A twig broke close by, followed by silence.

Someone was hiding in the bushes.

Without pausing to think, she did the first thing that came to mind. She screamed Zac's name as loud as she could.

The bushes erupted into crashing noises and grunts as if someone was attempting to push his way through the shrubs to the neighbor's yard. Olivia knew the hedge thinned a few feet further down from where she stood. Oblivious to the thorns and rocks biting at her bare feet, she arrived where the branches separated in time to see a man wearing a Seahawks jacket leap over the neighbor's fence. He carried something black in his right hand.

Footsteps came from behind and she whirled around to find Zac approaching. "That way," she yelled, pointing. "The man from the store. I think he has a gun."

Zac's eyes glistened in the light from the neighbor's porch. "Grant is behind your garage, unconscious. Get help," he said, and then he crashed through the bushes, running the direction she pointed, his own weapon drawn, his parting expression grim.

Grant was on the ground behind her garage unconscious? That made no sense to Olivia.

She had to get to her children. She wasn't sure what was going on, but the thought occurred to her that she'd left them to come back here. Had that been part of some master plan? Were all the bad guys in cahoots?

She tumbled out of the bushes into her own yard and into the arms of two startled firemen.

"My children—"

"They're across the street, they're okay."

"Grant Robinson is over there behind the garage. He needs attention."

"I'll go see to him," one firemen said, jogging off.

A shot rang out, then another, and Olivia froze again, heart suspended. She started shaking as the remaining fireman put a supportive arm around her. As she moved away, she looked back over her shoulder, straining for a glimpse of Zac. She wanted to follow him, she was scared to death those shots had been fired at him and not by him. But she had to see to her children first.

"Come along, ma'am," the fireman said. "Sheriff Bishop will get whoever did this."

If whoever did this didn't get Sheriff Bishop first.

THE FIRST SHOT hit a garbage can off to the left. The second one got a rock in front of Zac's foot. Not liking the odds, Zac zigzagged, but between garage lights, a full moon and clear skies, the alley was pretty well lit and his assailant had taken cover behind a garage a couple of houses down. When another bullet plugged the fence he was in the process of jumping, Zac dove behind a big stack of oak logs probably aging for next winter's firewood, and crouched low.

He didn't have a radio with him, but by now he

was sure his department was on the way. That meant Dilly and Hoopes and whoever else was on duty would be showing up damn soon. In fact, he could hear sirens screeching along the streets.

This had to be the guy who had attacked Olivia and was probably the same one who had run over his little sister. Leaving him for Dilly to collar rubbed Zac the wrong way. He wanted to take him himself.

The gunman fired off another shot and Zac marked the location. Dogs were barking up and down the alley now, confusing the issue somewhat but maybe their yapping could help as well as hinder.

With no holster and nowhere else to stick the gun, he wedged it in the back waist of his jeans. The outbuilding's roof dipped close to the top of the stack of logs. There was an outside chance he could get on top of that roof. Moving as far into the cover of the building as he could, he put a leg up to see how stable the stack was. Not bad. Taking a deep breath, he all but launched himself upward, momentum imperative to make it without falling, until he reached the top and jumped.

It was farther away than it had looked. His hands caught the edge, but just barely. He hung there a second, swinging, until he got his wits about him, then pulled himself up to the relative safety of the old wooden shingles.

The dogs were having a fit now. The gunman must have heard something because he fired off another round, more or less revealing his location.

Zac grinned. "Thanks," he whispered as he stood carefully, slowly, knowing he would be momentarily silhouetted against the semi-lit night. No time to dawdle.

He was in luck. Three rooftops in a row, apparently three small garages or outbuildings lined up as pretty as could be with what appeared to be a manageable distance between them. He counted to three, took another deep breath and started running, hoping all three roofs were as solid as the one he started out on or it was going to be a short trip.

The dogs sensing or hearing a man running across the buildings above their heads went wild. It was a cheering section down there. A few lights went on as irate owners awoke, and Zac knew he had to hurry. He made the first leap and landed on the second roof, slid a step, gathered himself and kept going, leaping onto the third roof a second later. This one was unexpectedly steep but smaller than the other two and he was lucky to grab the peak.

How much noise had he made? Was the gunman standing down there pointing a gun upward?

Zac took a second to catch his breath before

pulling his head up level with the steepest point and peering over.

A very high fence on three sides and the blank wall of the building Zac was on top of ringed a small yard down below. It wasn't a yard, Zac decided, looking closer, it was a pen for securing a motorcycle that was parked against one end.

It appeared the gunman had gotten himself trapped. He was standing against the gate, looking through the slats, his attention diverted out into the alley. The man squatted, stood, drummed his fingers against his thigh, ran his hand through his hair, shifted his weight back and forth from one foot to the other.

Zac caught the flashing red-and-blue lights of a squad car not fifty feet away. His men had obviously blocked both ends of the alley and were undoubtedly proceeding with a search. A slight shift in Zac's position and he could see an officer walking toward the pen, swinging a flashlight, weapon drawn. From the slight shape of him, it had to be Dilly. He was moments away from shining a light toward a nervous armed man who had nowhere else to go but past Dilly.

Dilly yelled a general warning about coming out with hands up. His voice reinvigorated the dogs. Zac used the ensuing noise to pull himself to the peak of the roof where he stood briefly. Dilly must have caught sight of him for his head jerked up. That alerted the gunman who swiveled around, his weapon now aimed at Zac. Zac took off down the roof at full tilt, leaping at the far edge, landing on the gunman as bullets rang out.

"IT LOOKS LIKE it was a couple of smoke bombs," the fireman said. "Homemade, we think. Big ones, though, thrown through the basement and the kitchen windows."

"Homemade?"

"Anyone can get the directions off the Internet. A little sugar, a little salt peter."

"And that can be found in fertilizer, I believe," Brad Makko said. He'd arrived a few moments before, parking on a side street and walking in to see if he could be of help. He said he heard all the sirens and had a feeling Olivia was involved because in his experience, Danny always left mayhem in his wake. No reason why the fact he was dead should change that. Olivia didn't have the slightest idea what to tell him to do, so she asked him to just stay close for a while, and he'd been great.

"That's right, potassium nitrate. Pop it all in a skillet, pour it into some foil, add a fuse. No big deal. We've set up big evacuation fans and the air is clearing fast. You ought to be able to go inside pretty soon."

"But not to stay," Olivia said. "Not until we make sure the air is safe for babies with premature lungs and not until the kitchen and basement windows are replaced."

"Sounds like a good idea."

Olivia looked over his shoulder as the ambulance crew rolled a gurney from around the side of the house, Grant Robinson's bulky form covered with a dull white blanket. She'd already heard Grant had been bopped over the head and left unconscious, but the EMTs had confided that they thought he'd be fine after a day or so. No one had any explanation of what he was doing in her yard in the middle of the night. Apparently, he wasn't talking yet.

Behind her, in the neighbor's house, her family either slept or rocked and comforted babies. Everyone was safe, but she could not stay inside with Zac chasing a gunman outside. Dogs howled and barked, police cars blocked the street as well as the alley, people were being warned to stay inside.

Another police car came through the roadblock. It pulled up even with Olivia and Brad Makko as the fireman excused himself to go help clean up.

The passenger door opened and Zac got out. Olivia was so glad to see him alive and apparently whole, that she hurried to him, feeling awkward and embarrassed and about to cry yet again, but unable to stay a discreet distance. He smiled at her and put his arm around her shoulders, hugging her soundly, and then, as though recalling what had happened between them, dropping his arm.

His chest was scraped as were his arms, but he looked pleased with himself and so handsome it made Olivia's breath catch. Why was she seeing him this way now, when it was too late? Had that kiss sensitized her to him in a physical way she hadn't know existed before?

"We got him," Zac said.

"Is he someone local?"

"I don't think so. He's not carrying identification and he's not talking. Dilly took him in to book him. I just wanted to come by here and get the rest of my clothes before I go in to interrogate him."

"Thank goodness it's over," Brad Makko said, running a tan hand through his fair hair. Olivia was touched to hear the relief in his voice. What must have it been like for him to follow in his brother's destructive wake all these years? There were so many questions she wanted to ask him.

"I need to get diapers and formula from the house and take it across the street, but the fans are still working," she said.

"I'll go in with you," Brad said.

"I'll go with you," Zac said firmly. "Are you bringing the kids back tonight?"

"No, the neighbors have offered room. The firemen

said we could come back home, but I want to make sure the air is clear."

"And the windows are fixed," Brad chimed in.

Olivia turned to Brad. "Would you go across the street and tell my family I'll be there with supplies in a few minutes?"

"Sure," he said enthusiastically. "Are you sure you don't need help carrying things?"

"Zac will help me."

She and Zac went through the front door into the living room. The house had a faint smell of smoke, kind of like after a Fourth of July fireworks party. Not bad. Zac grabbed his shirt off the couch.

"You heard what the firemen found?"

He pulled the shirt over his head. "Homemade smoke bombs? Yeah. They took what remained of them. We'll get an expert to look it over."

"The man you chased down tonight must have made it."

"I agree. If we find the raw materials when we search his place, then we'll know for sure."

"Except what was Grant doing there?"

"I have no idea."

"Know what?" Olivia said, walking into the nursery. "It all seems like a big disjointed mess to me. Why would a man with a gun lob a firebomb into a house?"

"To empty the house so he could get inside," he said, leaning against the doorjamb.

"Didn't he think about the fire trucks responding?"

"I don't know, I'll ask him. Obviously, he didn't know about the other alarm. Think of it this way. If he used a long fuse and was poised to enter the house as soon as you heard the fire alarm go off, he'd have until the fire department responded to get inside and search. Maybe he knew exactly what he wanted."

"He would be the only one who did," she quipped.

"The alarm company hooked up the intruder alarm to the police and fire departments. The moment the window broke, the alarms went off and the clock started ticking. It probably scared him back into the bushes where he waited to see if there'd be an opportunity later for him to enter."

"And then I scared him away by stopping right by the bushes, right in front of him. I stood there for a while. It must have spooked him."

"Why did you stand there, Olivia? What were you doing in the back, anyway?"

"I thought you called me," she said.

"Nope."

"I just keep wondering why Grant was back there."

"He's got some explaining to do. I still don't get why you stopped by the hedge."

She had collected a stack of diapers and was filling a cloth bag with other necessities when she glanced up and saw the porcelain figurine that resembled Faith staring down at her.

She looked at Zac, who regarded her with his intense blue stare. "I saw you leaning over Grant only I didn't know it was Grant. I just couldn't move."

"Why?" he said, standing upright and taking a step into the room.

"I—" She rubbed her forehead and closed her eyes a second. Glancing back at him, she said, "I felt so terrible about earlier tonight."

He stared into her eyes for a second, then smiled. "Don't worry about it."

"I behaved crazy, even for me."

This earned her a more genuine smile. "I didn't behave all that well myself."

"The truth is I do know—"

This time he held up a hand to still her. "The truth is neither one of us has had a decent night's sleep in so long it doesn't count. This mess tonight added on to everything that's happened today is just too much for either of us to handle. You asked tonight if we could still be friends."

"And you didn't answer."

"I'm answering now. Sure, we can be friends. Just like always. No big deal."

"But Zac, you should know, the truth is I have been thinking about you, about us, too. It just scares me."

He took another step and touched her cheek. He'd touched her cheek a million times before, but this time the feel of his fingers running along her jaw sent shivers through her face, racing down her arms and back. He withdrew his hand at once. He looked tired and battered and she longed to comfort him. She put a finger on his chin where a knife had sliced through the skin a dozen years before and tele-graphed a message to him. *Help me get past my fear, help me!*

He caught her hand and lowered it. "It's okay. The fact is the thought of you and me scares me, too. It was all just a giant misunderstanding. A mistake."

Not what she wanted him to say. Why wasn't he a mind reader? "Okay," she said. She glanced back at the figurine and said, "Have you heard anything from the hospital?"

"I'm going to call them now while you get the rest of what you need."

STRIPPED OF HIS PADDED JACKET, the gunman turned out to be a six-foot-four, one-hundred-and-ninety-pound white man with very curly light brown hair, brown eyes and three healing scratches down his left cheek, plus the remainder of a shiner over his left eye. These old injuries begged the question: Were they the remnants of the fight he and Danny Makko, aka Anthony Capri, had staged in Olivia's house the night Danny was killed? They fingerprinted him and ran it through the system.

Jed Palmer, aka Twitch, wanted for questioning in a carjack and a robbery, outstanding warrants for DUI and assault. Thirty-four years old. Address, Seattle.

Twitch tapped his toes, thumped his fingers against the table and chatted up a blue streak about nothing except wanting his lawyer. Hence he was a guest in the cell block while the process of getting blood and DNA samples to match to the spatters in Olivia's home and to the skin found beneath Danny Marko's fingernails was started.

"You still going to Seattle?" Dilly asked, setting a cup of coffee down in front of Zac.

Zac picked up the cup, stared at the sludge within and put it back down. "I'm going to the hospital first and make sure Faith is okay. The news on the phone was no change, but if I get over there about seven, I can talk to her doctor and check on Dad. Oh, and stop by Grant Robinson's room. He better have a damn good excuse for being in Olivia's backyard in the middle of the night."

He glanced up at the clock. It never ceased to amaze him how fast time could speed by when hell came a knockin'.

Dilly said, "I sure hope Faith makes it, Zac."

"She will. She has to. If she's holding her own, I'll go. If she's not, then I'll call and see if I can cancel the trial and you can go meet Dave. I want to talk to Makko's brother, too, and he made noise about leaving today."

"We heard back from Vegas, by the way. Brad Makko, married to Maria Makko, brother Danny no one has seen for years. Still working on Lindy Makko's whereabouts."

"Call me as soon as you hear anything. Go by the hotel and take a statement from Brad Makko. Find out anything you can about Danny and make sure we have a contact address for Brad. If he could possibly stick around an extra day, that would be great. If he can, make an appointment for me to talk to him this afternoon. No. On second thought, make it for this evening so you and I can compare notes first."

"What about the gamblers who showed up on Olivia's doorstep?"

"Yeah, what about them? Why didn't they show up last night? I'm hoping Seattle will have information on them, too. I haven't called my old partner, too much has been going on, but I'll stop by after the trial. We know Twitch has connections in Seattle. Him being down here and standing outside Olivia's house with a gun can't be a coincidence." He scanned a sheet of paper and said, "You get someone to tow in Twitch's car?"

"Yeah, we found it parked two blocks over. Big old dark blue thing. I'm making a cast of the tires later. By the way, I have Twitch's weapon. Same caliber as plugged Capri, I mean Makko. We'll get it to the lab for ballistic tests."

"Good. Get the shop to look for evidence of a hit-and-run on that car. It matches the general description for the vehicle that ran down Faith."

"Already on it."

Zac grunted approval as he gathered a stack of papers together and stuck them in his briefcase. "You can hold down the fort for a few hours?"

"Absolutely. Call if the plans change. Thanks, by the way, for taking on Twitch. I have a feeling I'd be full of holes if you hadn't jumped on him."

Zac smiled. "Happy to do it. Keep someone patrolling Olivia's neighborhood, okay?"

"You got it."

ZAC DROVE to his house first, taking time to shower, shave, and put on fresh clothes. He'd caught a couple of hours' sleep in his office and didn't feel half as tired as he deserved to feel, but he was stiff and his side hurt. A brief examination in the mirror and he knew he could expect bruises up and down his side by nightfall.

Dressed in his gray suit and a tie Faith had given him for his last birthday, he paused in the kitchen to make toast and drink a glass of orange juice. He'd bought the one-story house when he got married. His ex-wife had lived in it for exactly sixteen months and three days before tearfully admitting she hated Westerly. In fact, she hated the Pacific Northwest, and she wasn't all that fond of him. She accused him of not loving her and he'd been flabbergasted until about a month after she left when he realized she'd been absolutely right.

He'd married her because it had seemed the right time to settle down. She'd been a lot of fun and just as clueless as he'd been. He hadn't loved her, though, not in the way he now knew love could be. There hadn't been the extremes, the tension, the euphoria, the need, the ache for her.

So, he'd kept the house because it was located close to the river and was shaded in the summer by sweeping oak trees, because it was roomy and set up well and because, face it, Olivia had once walked through the place and told him she loved it.

Was it a coincidence that he'd married when Olivia went away to college and lost his wife the month Olivia came back home after her father died?

He didn't know if his feelings had been growing for that long, he just wasn't sure.

Anyway, now he would let the house go. He'd envisioned Olivia in the place too many times, he'd heard her babies—the children he'd dreamed of adopting and raising as his own—playing in the bedrooms, giggling from the backyard. He had to let go. Maybe he'd buy one of the new condos downtown.

First things first. He had to make sure Olivia and her family were safe and though his gut told him they had Anthony's killer—okay, Danny Makko's killer—behind bars, there were still too many loose ends. He wanted to know where those gamblers had disappeared to and he wanted to know what was going on with Grant Robinson.

And he had to make sure Faith woke up.

Breakfast over, he drove to the hospital.

Olivia was sitting in the lobby. She stood as he came through the door. She wore black slacks, a black sweater and a black eye. Nevertheless, she looked pretty well-rested considering everything and as sexy as she always did, though there was a new maturity in her face and a haunted look in her eyes.

But the bottom line for him was that—judging by the quickening of his pulse and the thinning of his blood when he looked at her—there would never be peace for him in her company.

She looked away from his gaze. He made a conscious effort to act casual just as he had back in her house a few hours earlier when he'd watched her pack diapers. They had to stay close until this situation was resolved, he couldn't afford for her to be so uneasy around him that she stopped talking to him.

"I came to see Faith. I figured you'd show up. Is it okay if I go in with you?" she added, casting him a swift glance.

"Of course it is. It'll be good for her to hear your voice."

"I also wanted to know if that man you arrested is Anthony's killer. Danny's killer. I can't get used to that name."

"I don't know for sure. He isn't talking. We'll put him in a lineup later, and you can come in and see if something clicks. I took a recording of his voice. He's just rambling and it won't be admissible in court, but if you listen to it, it might help."

"The man at the convenience store said he shot Danny."

"I know. My gut feeling is we have him. We'll go at him again this afternoon after he's had a chance to talk to a lawyer. If he isn't the killer he may be willing to point a finger. Meanwhile, Dilly is working on tracking down Danny Makko's wife so we can get a better idea of his past and where he might have been wiring money."

"And what about Grant?"

"He has some questions to answer." He glanced at his watch. "I have to be in Seattle for a court date. Let's go see Faith. I don't want to miss her doctor."

He punched off his phone in the elevator, which kept his hands busy so he wasn't tempted to grab Olivia's elbow or offer her a supporting arm. His body ached with awareness of her, though, and he averted his gaze, steeling himself for the years ahead. He wouldn't leave Westerly this time, but he would change his life to include different people. It was the only way he could remain sane.

They were allowed into the ICU, though technically that would put too many people in Faith's cubicle. It helped to be sheriff.

Faith's head was bandaged and her eyes were closed. The facial cuts had been taped as had her hands, which she'd cut when she skidded on them. One leg was in a cast as was one arm. She was hooked up to a half dozen monitors all beeping at different tempos like a shrill band gone mad.

His old man looked absolutely worn to a frazzle but he stood immediately and hugged Olivia.

"Hey, Dad," Zac said, clapping his father gently on the back. "How's she doing?"

"'Bout the same," Gus said, covering a yawn with his hand.

"Why don't you go get a cup of coffee and something to eat? We'll stay with Faith until the doctor comes."

"I think I'll stop by the chapel," he said, and left, his back more bent than Zac had seen it before. He was afraid if Faith didn't recover, she wasn't going to be the only casualty of the hit-and-run. Zac's desire to go back to the jail and beat a confession out of Twitch all but consumed him.

He turned back into the room to find that Olivia had taken the chair his father had just vacated. She sat near Faith's head and he watched as Olivia took a small figurine of a woman doing a curtsey from her huge handbag and set it on the tray facing Faith.

"She's going to watch over you for me," Olivia whispered, "because I can't stay here with you like I want to. I have to take care of the babies, you understand, don't you, Faith?" As she spoke, she ran her hand up and down Faith's uninjured arm.

These were the two most important women in his life and the thought he could lose both of them just about undid Zac. His jaw knotted as he leaned against the wall and listened to Olivia's soothing voice, so full of love it was like a song. He tried to let it soothe him, as well, but face it, nothing about Olivia at the moment calmed him.

He heard quiet footsteps and turned to find Faith's doctor standing in the door. She was a woman of about forty with short dark hair and earnest brown eyes behind thick glasses. She wasn't much taller than his sister, but she carried herself as though she was a giant.

"I looked over her chart," she said, addressing Zac.

"And?"

"And I'm optimistic."

"Has she woken up yet?"

"No." The doctor stared at Faith and Olivia for a moment, then added, "That's not unusual given what she went through. But her vitals are better. She's running a slight fever, so we'll keep an eye on that, but there's no indication she's still bleeding internally. I'm not going to say she's out of the woods, I'm just saying there's hope."

"When she recovers will there be any permanent damage?" Zac asked quietly, hoping to spare Olivia.

The doctor met his gaze. "I don't know. It's borrowing trouble to speculate at this point, you understand?"

"Yes. Of course. My dad—"

"Needs to go home and get some sleep."

"I'll spell him. I think he'd leave if I stayed here with Faith."

"There's nothing either one of you can do." She glanced at Olivia, then back at him. "I heard about what happened last night. It's all over town. You have work to do. Go do it."

"I'll see," Zac said.

"Try not to worry. Faith is a healthy young woman. Give her time."

Olivia moved out of the way as the doctor did a brief examination. After she left, Zac sat next to his sister for a few moments, willing her strength, wondering how he could get out of the court date, when a small commotion outside the room caught both his and Olivia's attention and they went to investigate.

They found Olivia's mother with her arm through Zac's father's arm. The nurse had put her foot down as to the number of visitors so they all left the immediate area and gathered in the ICU waiting room.

"I found this handsome guy drinking coffee by himself," Juliet Hart said. She looked like an older version of Olivia. The Hart women swam in a good gene pool.

Olivia said, "The babies—"

"Are fine. They're still at Charlie and Velma's house with your sisters, waiting for you to come get them and take them home. Tabitha has a physics test this afternoon she shouldn't miss. Charlie is sitting on the front porch with a shotgun. I finally got smart and phoned in a grocery order to the store. It arrived and it's all put away. The glass-repair people have come and gone from your house, the fire department says your air is just fine, the appraiser called and said he'll be here at noon, what's-his-name, Anthony's brother, he called. He's coming over when you give him the word. I'm taking a few hours off to sit with Faith so Gus can go home and eat something and sleep for a while so he doesn't scare the living daylights out of his daughter when she wakes up. I know Zac has a court date in Seattle. Everyone scoot."

And just like that, everyone was doing exactly what Juliet wanted with the exception that Zac had walked Olivia and his father to her car—she was giving the old man a lift—and then detoured back inside the hospital to pay a visit to Grant Robinson. He'd left both his father and Olivia with stern warnings to lock doors and stay alert, there were still unaccounted for bad guys and agendas floating around and so far their only suspect in custody wasn't talking.

Maybe Grant would shed a little much needed light.

Grant was in the process of getting dressed when Zac rapped on his door. It was Hugh who let Zac in.

As Grant laced up his boots, Zac got a good look

at him. He'd known him most of his life—Westerly was like that. As long as Zac had known the older man, he'd been wealthy and belligerent, not a great combination. It wasn't too hard to imagine Grant pulling a sophomoric trick like lobbing smoke bombs through Olivia's windows but how that tied into Twitch was unclear. Unless Grant and Twitch were in cahoots.

Right now, true to form with everyone else, Grant had a bandage on his head and a cut across his left cheek. Hugh had a shiner. It seemed everyone in town was currently black and blue.

Hugh said, "I guess you came to arrest me."

Zac flicked his gaze from Grant to Hugh. He'd had his worries about Grant and the fact he'd been caught on the same piece of illicit real estate as Twitch, but what was Hugh talking about?

Hugh held his hands out in front of himself. "Go on, cuff me."

"Why would I cuff you?"

"Just do it," Grant huffed. He finished lacing his boots and stood stiffly. Zac recognized the same grass-stained chinos and plaid shirt with blood spattered down the front as from the night before. Apparently, Hugh had not brought his brother fresh clothes.

"You guys are losing me. I came here to find out

what the hell you were doing out behind Olivia's house last night."

Grant said, "I was going over there to talk to her. I want my money back."

"You know she doesn't have that money," Hugh said a little wearily.

"I don't know nothing of the sort," Grant insisted. "She told the whole world she was Anthony's partner."

"She got goaded into that by a reporter," Hugh said. "Everyone else has figured that out, why can't you?"

Zac held up a hand. "Wait a second. What's going on?"

"My brother is a jackass," Hugh said with an impatient flick of his wrist.

Zac sat on the edge of the window sill. A glance at his watch told him he had to hurry these two along. "Tell me why you were in Olivia's yard and why you think I should arrest either one of you. For now, give me the short version."

They both stared at the floor for a while. Zac said, "I have half a mind to arrest both of you and sort it out later."

Grant grunted, stubborn to the last.

Hugh said, "At first I thought my brother had left the house to go for a drive to cool down."

"We got a call from our accountant yesterday," Grant grumbled.

"We've decided to sue Anthony Capri's estate and that's when we got into an argument about how deep Olivia was into the whole thing," Hugh added. "Like I said, Grant stormed off. I went looking for him a while later. He hadn't taken his truck. There was a cold wind blowing and he hadn't put on a jacket so I didn't think he'd gone far. I got to wondering if he had headed on over to bother Olivia."

"Four tiny babies and a dead husband, what do you expect, she's sleeping?" Grant said. "I was just going to go talk to her."

"I caught up with him behind her house. There's a path back there going through the alleys—"

"I was having second thoughts because the place was so dark," Grant said.

"We got into another argument."

"To make a long story short," Grant said, "Hugh hit me on the head with a rock."

"Actually, I used a brick I found laying on the ground after you knocked me down first," Hugh said, eyes flashing.

"And then?" Zac prompted.

"Then all hell broke loose," Hugh said. "I saw a man run up to the house and throw something, I heard glass break and then the alarms went off and a minute later, you came running around the corner from the front and I couldn't rouse Grant, so I decided to cut my losses and go home."

"My brother, the hero," Grant said. "Left me there to die. Go ahead, arrest him."

"A simple blow to the head couldn't kill you," Hugh scoffed. "There's nothing up there to hurt."

"Are you filing charges?" Zac asked Grant.

Grant glared at his brother and then shook his graying head. "No."

"Well, if Olivia doesn't file trespassing charges, I have nothing to arrest you for. Yet. But it looks mighty suspicious you were back there at the same time Jed Palmer was causing havoc. If I find out you two hired that man to terrorize Olivia and her family, I will personally get the DA to throw the book at you. And if you hired him to kill the man you knew as Anthony Capri, you're both toast. Now, I'm going to call Dilly who will get someone over here to take you two to the station to make statements. I'm asking you to go of your own free will and I'm warning you not to leave town. If you refuse, we'll get a warrant. Are we clear? Oh, and one more thing. Under no circumstances are either one of you to contact Olivia Capri. Stay away from her."

"You got the hots for that little gal?" Grant said.

Zac clenched his jaw and stared hard at Grant. "Are you blind?" he asked. "Has it completely escaped your notice that Olivia has been the target of one jerk after another? That her house has been broken into, her children threatened? You've been running around town bad-mouthing her because of something she said in a moment of panic while trying to defend a man who wasn't really her husband. Did it ever occur to you that she's more a victim than either one of you will ever be? So you got greedy and lost a couple of million. You've got millions more and you know it. But Olivia lost damn near everything, plus she's going to have one hell of a hospital bill to settle up in Seattle. I hope she figures out a way to sue you for defamation of character." He took a deep breath before adding, "Grant, why didn't you come into my office and see me yesterday morning? You told Detective Dilly that was your plan."

Grant shrugged beefy shoulders. "I changed my mind."

"Wait here until one of my men comes."

"But I brought my car," Hugh protested.

"You can get it later. I strongly urge you to follow directions. You don't need more trouble. Think about what I said."

Chapter Ten

Olivia dropped Zac's father off at his house, waiting until he'd gone inside and locked the door. She drove home half-distracted, her heart heavy in her chest.

Faith had been so still, so vulnerable, Zac had been so restrained, Gus had been so discouraged. Thank goodness for her take-no-prisoners mother.

They spent the next couple of hours getting the babies settled. Olivia had called Brad and asked him to come over later, but he'd said he had nothing to do, he was tired of sitting around the hotel or driving around town, would she mind if he came early and spent some time with her and the babies. As she had quickly learned the mother of quads was a fool to turn down a pair of willing hands, she said sure.

When the phone rang after speaking with Brad, she assumed it was him calling her back. The caller ID blocked the name and number.

The voice who responded to her greeting, however,

wasn't that of Brad Makko, though it did sound remotely familiar.

"You remember me?" the man said.

"I'm sorry," Olivia responded. Maybe it was the appraiser. She said, "Is this Mr. Lawrence?"

"Me and a couple of my friends came to see you two nights ago. Now you remember?"

An image of a knife flashed in her mind. "You're the tall one. The man with you, Shorty, had a knife."

"Very good. We've been watching your place, Mrs. Capri. It's like Grand Central Station around there."

"Are you behind what's been happening? You and the others or your so-called boss?"

"Not us. All we want is our fifty grand. You find the goods?"

"What goods?" she snapped. "I don't have the slightest idea—"

"Now you listen here—"

"No, you listen," Olivia said, anger encroaching on fear. "I'm sick of this game you're playing. I don't know if you killed Anthony or you hired someone else to do it. And if you ran down Faith—"

"Now wait just a second. All we want is our money. You bring the goods to Seattle—"

"I thought you were coming here to collect."

"You've got cops hanging around twenty-four-seven, lady. No way we're coming there. You bring it here."

"Bring what?"

"What you and your husband—"

"You know what? Turns out he wasn't my husband."

A long pause was followed with, "I want you to remember that sooner or later the cops will move on to bigger and better things and Shorty still has his knife."

Olivia slammed down the receiver.

A knock on the door a few feet away made her jump. She looked through the peephole to see Brad Makko standing on the step and opened the door quickly. He took one look at her and said, "Oh, my God, what's happened now?"

She looked over his shoulder, up and down the street, relieved when Deputy Kellerman pulled up in front of her house.

"Come inside," she told Brad. "I'll tell you what's going on."

EVENTUALLY, Sandy left to take Brianna to the rescheduled pediatrician appointment. It felt so odd to have her sister leave with one of her babies, climbing into the backseat of Kellerman's police unit. Two women from the pharmacy showed up to help with a feeding and life settled into a chaotic kind of schedule Olivia wondered if she would ever get used to. The involvement with her children drove some of the craziness aside, but she had to stop herself over and over again from calling Zac on his cell.

The dream was to have the babies all to herself, but how possible was that dream given the circumstances? Maybe the mother of a single child could be the center of the universe to her first baby, maybe she could take the time to do everything for her child, but the mother of four didn't have that kind of luxury.

She and Brad finally sat down in the basement, the boxes between them. "This first box holds the items Zac and I thought might have some sort of value. The appraiser will be here shortly, I was just wondering what you remembered of these things, if anything at all."

"Are you trying to get enough money together to pay off the gamblers who have been threatening you?"

"I don't think anything that was once your brother's is now mine. Maybe they were never legally his. I just want whatever it is out of my house. Then I'll take out a big ad announcing I'm bankrupt."

Chuckling, he picked up a stack of baseball cards. "Well, let's see. Danny collected cards as a kid. Baseball, football. I have no idea if any of these are valuable. How much did you say those gamblers demanded?"

"Fifty thousand."

"That's a lot of money. Hard to imagine it's in a sports card."

She picked up the small landscape to show him, pausing for a second. "Brad, can you tell me why Danny went through the motions of pretending to marry me? I mean, if he was already married, why fake a new relationship?"

Brad put the cards back in the plastic box in which they'd been stored. "Well, looking at you, I think it's entirely possible he fell in love with you. He couldn't very well tell you the truth, could he?"

"No."

He smoothed his clipped mustache, a nervous gesture, or maybe one to stall for time before finally adding, "The truth? Danny once told me having a wife made him look more legitimate. You know, in business deals. He thought people wouldn't question his character so quickly if he had a wife and a home and all that."

Why it should hurt to hear this, Olivia wasn't sure. She didn't love the man she'd known as Anthony, she wasn't that big a fool. But when she thought of how blithely she'd believed what he told her, she felt ashamed of herself. Why had she fallen for his lies?

Because she'd wanted out of Westerly, she'd wanted to travel, she'd had dreams and he'd sensed them and fed them back to her as his own.

"Then tell me this," she said softly. "When he found out I was having quadruplets he was obviously upset. He started staying away from home more, but he still went through the motions. He lied to me about the house being ready when it was never really going to be our house."

"That big old place out on the sound? I swear you can see Canada from the deck."

"You've been there?"

"Drove out there early this morning," Brad said. "I couldn't sleep after all the excitement last night. Watched the sun come up over the mountains. The place appears to be abandoned."

"It is. It belongs to the bank now."

"It's got its own dock, did you know that?"

"No. I heard it was in the plans to dredge a marina, but that was probably never going to happen."

"Well this has a nice little dock."

"It was foggy when I went." Her voice faltered for a second—the last time she'd been there she'd been with Zac and had found Brad's brother buried in the garage.

Brad shook his head. "It seems to me my brother had everything."

"On the surface," she said. "Deep down where it mattered, he didn't have anything."

"True. Did he ever talk about me in any way, like maybe his visit to Vegas? We did some exciting things when he was there, went to a few fancy parties, had some laughs."

She could see how important it was to him, but he kept stressing honesty with her and so she replied in kind. "No, I'm sorry."

"I just wondered if whatever he's been selling off was connected to Vegas or maybe to California, where he went before he came up here."

"I have no way of knowing the validity of anything he told me. If there were kernels of truth in with the lies, I wouldn't know. After I wound up in the hospital in Seattle, he started gambling, and that gambling apparently led to everything that's happening now. If he had something valuable squirreled away here, why not just take it and run?"

"And nobody knows what it is?"

"Someone must, but every time someone tells me to find 'it', they just tell me I'll know if I see it. I don't think they know for sure and the police are looking for the guy who fenced the stuff, but that doesn't seem promising."

"I just never knew Danny to actually steal anything," he said. "I mean outright take a candy bar off a shelf, that kind of thing. Did he ever mention stealing?"

"No, but the truth is he stole millions," she reminded him.

Brad clamped his hands between his knees and studied the toes of his pricey boots. "Danny had a gambling addiction, that's for sure. Not the kind where he gambled every day, the kind that might go years where he didn't do any at all then he'd fall hard off the wagon." He looked at her through eyes that looked so much like Danny's. "So, the gambling part I get. As for not running away at the get-go and stringing you along—well, from what I gather, he was in the middle of conning people and wiring money to a new identity, so I guess he couldn't leave until that part was done. Plus, again, maybe he had genuine feelings for you."

"I don't think so."

Brad shook his head. "I'm sorry I can't be of more help. I never understood my brother. Never."

"It's okay. It's just been bothering me." She handed him the painting in the gold frame, once again impressed by the rich colors, the bold brush strokes.

He peered at the signature. "I can't read this."

"I can't either. Is the painting itself familiar?"

He pursed his lips, then shook his head. "No. Pretty little scene though, isn't it?"

"Yes." She took it back and set it in the box.

Upstairs, she heard the doorbell ring and glanced at her watch. "That's the appraiser."

"Do you want me to keep going through these things while you talk to him?"

"No, this is something I have to do, but you're welcome to stay. I guess all this stuff belongs to Lindy Makko. Maybe you could give me her Texas address so I could send it to her."

"Sure."

She paused for a second and added, "When your brother's body is released, I think you or his wife should see to his burial."

"Yes," he said. "I've been reluctant to bring it up. I'll talk to someone about that."

She nodded briskly and got to her feet. They walked up the stairs, but it was just Sandy who had forgotten to take a house key. Deputy Kellerman was standing in the room with her and it was he who held Brianna, a big smile on his usually somber face. Sandy squealed when she saw Olivia. "She gained two whole ounces!"

Considering the baby seemed to spit up her weight every day, they all oohed and aahed while Brad produced a disposable camera and snapped a few pictures. Olivia took Brianna and pretended she was almost too heavy to lift, and they laughed some more. It was as though this minor piece of good news displaced some of the horror of the last two days, and Olivia cuddled her smallest child as close as she could.

It was Sandy who answered the next knock to a small man with watery eyes holding a blue bandana in one hand and a briefcase in the other.

"Mr. Lawrence," Olivia said. "Please come in."

Lawrence shook off a sneeze. "Your street is lined with maple trees, the wind is blowing and I'm allergic," he said, and in the next moment sneezed two times. "Let me inside."

"I'm sorry, please come in."

He held up a hand and sneezed again. "It's no better in here. Let's get this over with," he said, looking from face to face.

As Brad Makko led Lawrence down the stairs, Olivia said a hasty good-bye to Tabitha, who had to leave for her physics test, and reluctantly handed Brianna back to Sandy. "The hardware ladies are coming pretty soon to help you and Megan?"

"Don't worry about a thing. Just get this figured out so we can all breathe easier, okay?"

"I'll try."

What would she do without her family? she wondered as she started down the stairs. Her step faltered as she thought of Faith, still unconscious. And then her grip on the handrail tightened as the impressions from the morning came skittering into her head. They'd been driven away by the threatening phone call and the babies' needs and Brad's revelations, but they were back now. Zac hadn't touched her that morning, had barely looked her in the eye. He'd been pleasant but not warm.

Her stomach clenched as tears stung behind her nose.

He was leaving her in every way that counted.

And who could blame him?

THE TRIAL was a miracle in that Zac arrived on schedule, testified promptly and was relieved. In all his time as a city cop, it had never gone that smoothly.

He met up with his ex-partner a half hour later.

Dave O'Sullivan was a tall man of about forty-five with still vibrant thick red hair. He favored jeans and white shirts and always looked ready to stop by a tavern and play a round of pool.

"You got yourself a mess down there in Westerly," Dave said.

"Tell me about it," Zac replied. As usual around Dave, he felt overdressed.

Dave stood up and offered a hearty handshake. "Your timing is impeccable as usual," he said. "I recognized the guys in the drawings you faxed me. Arrested two of them last night as a matter of fact. The third one is less than three miles from here and I was about to go talk to him. His name is Sam Barber. Want to come with me?"

Zac glanced at his watch. He'd called the

hospital—no change with Faith—and he'd called Dilly who reported things were quiet at Olivia's house and that Kellerman had more or less moved in. He hadn't been able to bring himself to call Olivia directly. He liked to think of himself as a brave man but right now he'd rather dive into shark infested waters than talk to Olivia. "Sure."

Dave grabbed a denim jacket off the back of his chair. "Let's go."

Sam Barber turned out to be exactly what his name portended: a barber who cut hair down near the waterfront in a little hole in the wall place.

They found Sam seated in his barber chair. His smile of shocked welcome—how often did a stranger actually come in here for a haircut?—dissipated as he caught sight of Dave.

"Whatever it is, I didn't do it," Sam said. He was a heavyset man with a receding hairline and a long nose. Sara Hoopes had caught his image very well.

"I just want to introduce you to the sheriff from down in Westerly, Sam. This is Zac Bishop. He's good friends with a lady named Olivia Capri. You remember her?"

Sam's expression immediately turned shifty-eyed as he stared at magazines, newspapers, anything but at Zac. He said, "No, I don't think so."

"You showed up at her door with a guy named Shorty and a sandy-haired guy," Zac said. "Two nights ago. You threatened to carve her into pieces if she didn't cooperate."

"No. No, I've had the flu—" He coughed to prove it.

Zac crossed his arms and narrowed his eyes. "What kind of car do you drive, Sam?"

"Me? I don't have a car—"

"Because someone in a dark sedan ran down my sister the next day."

"I told you, I don't have a car."

"Olivia saw you get in a dark sedan."

"That's Cash's car."

"If you were in it at the time—"

"Cash didn't do it, either. We're not fiends. Well, maybe Shorty is…"

Zac waved Barber off. "Just book him, Dave. I'll get Twitch to talk about Mr. Barber's involvement with the murder."

"Wait a second," Sam Barber said, springing from the chair like it was suddenly on fire. "The Capri broad traced my call this morning, didn't she? Damn her."

"What call?" Zac said calmly, but his gut twisted.

"I just called her, friendly like. She's got some attitude."

Zac said, "This is a waste of time, Dave. I'll talk to Twitch."

"Now wait a second," Barber said. "Listen, I got nothing to do with Twitch."

"Did he have anything to do with your boss?"

"He hung around Pike, sure, but—"

"That would be Berry Pike," Dave explained to Zac. "I arrested him last night. He was running an illegal operation on the north side. He's going to be busy doing time for the next couple of years." He turned back to Barber and added, "We got your pals Shorty and Cash, too, and your name came up."

"Sounds like Barry Pike was the boss you told Olivia about," Zac said.

"Now wait a second—" Barber said.

Dave ignored him. "So the dead man reneged on a gambling debt and Sam and his buddies killed him for it?"

Zac slid Barber a steely-eyed, challenging look and said, "Maybe."

"No, now, just wait. Why would Pike or me or the guys kill Capri? His death got us nothing. He'd owed us before and he'd come through. We knew he'd come through again."

"By fencing something."

"Yeah."

"That he took from his house?"

"We didn't know that until after he got himself killed and then it was in the papers that there was blood at his place."

"But Twitch didn't work for you or Pike?"

"No way. The guy's bad news. Jumpy, that's why

they call him Twitch. Always hanging back like one of them hyenas, looking for a way to make a buck.'

"Where did Capri fence things?"

"I have no idea."

Dave said, "I've heard enough." He cuffed Barber, took out his phone and called the station. As he talked, Zac cozied up to Sam. "Tell me who the fence is. I won't mention your name."

"Why should I?"

"Because maybe he can help pin it on Twitch. Better to go to jail for a year or two than stand trial for murder, right?"

"I didn't kill no one—"

"So you say. It's hard to tell what Twitch's story will be after he talks with his lawyer. He's a known associate of yours, you've been recognized as one of the men who showed up after the murder—"

"Okay, okay!" Barber chewed the inside of his lip for a second. "Go see Jenks down on Bay Street," he whispered. "If it's not him, he might know who to finger."

"Thank you." Zac caught Dave's eye and mouthed a "Later."

"THAT SCRAWL YOU CAN'T READ is an artist named James Reaper. The guy can paint a great sky." The appraiser stopped for a moment to sneeze and blow his nose and Olivia realized a window was open on the top of the locked screen door. She closed it as

Lawrence added, "I think this little painting is probably worth five, maybe six thousand. At an auction, mind you, to the right collector. On the street, maybe two or three."

"Not fifty," Olivia said, sitting down again.

"Not even close."

"And the cards?" Brad asked.

"No. Sorry, nothing worth that kind of cash. Maybe a couple hundred, again, to the right market on the right day."

Olivia heaved a huge sigh. He'd looked through everything else, discarding it all as nice but not really valuable. "How about porcelain figurines?" Olivia said.

"What figurines?" Lawrence sniffed.

"I have five little figurines Mr. Makko's mother collected."

Brad said, "They can't be worth much, Olivia. They're just worthless mementos."

"I know, but I thought—"

The appraiser dabbed at his eyes. "I...I..." he sneezed, and cleared his throat before ending, "might as well take a look—"

"I'll get them," Olivia said, standing. She scooped up an empty box and added, "They're in with the babies."

While Lawrence sneezed up a storm, she walked up the stairs and entered the nursery. A harried Sandy held the box as Olivia took the figurines off the top of the armoire and set them carefully inside. "I thought Lori and Paty from the pharmacy were coming to help with the feedings," Olivia said, her voice raised a bit to be heard over fussing babies.

"They were, but Paty texted me a few minutes ago. They're going to be late. Go finish up. I can keep the babies happy for another fifteen or twenty minutes."

"Okay, we're almost done."

She turned to find Brad Makko standing in the doorway.

"What a cute nursery," he said. "This is the first time I've actually seen it." He snapped a photo or two while he spoke.

"Really? I didn't know that."

"Very charming." His gaze roamed the entire room before landing once again on her. "I thought you might need help," he said, holding out his arms.

She handed him the box and he glanced inside. "I thought you said there were five of the little dolls. I only see four."

"It's a long story," she said.

He turned away and she followed him down the stairs.

Chapter Eleven

Zac entered Jenk's pawn shop as a woman shepard-
ing a three-year-old departed. The child had a long,
dark ponytail and big brown eyes and for just a
second, a sense of loss washed through him like a
tidal wave. Someday Olivia's girls would look much
like this child, only there would be four of them.

And he wouldn't be part of their lives.

He felt a great need to get back to Westerly, a
churning in his gut. Was the worry directed toward
Olivia or Faith or both of them? He couldn't tell, just
knew it was getting worse as the hours passed.

He needed to collect damning information to
throw at Twitch to get him to talk. If he was working
for someone, Zac wanted to know who. Maybe it
was Sam Barber and his friends, maybe Pike was
involved, maybe Grant and Hugh—whoever, it just
had to get resolved.

The cluttered, dusty shop didn't look any different than it had the first time Zac had been there, a

good six months earlier. For that matter, it didn't look as though it had been mucked out since the 1962 Seattle World's Fair.

"Hey, Jenks," Zac said, leaning on the counter.

Jenks, who had to be about sixty but looked eighty, regarded Zac with deeply hooded eyes. "I heard you left town."

"I'm back for a visit."

"And decided to stop in here?" Jenks said, his voice wry.

"I like your place, Jenks. It's colorful." Zac gazed into the gloom for a few moments before adding, "Have you been keeping up with the murder of that con man down in Westerly?"

"Can't say as I have."

"The man whose wife had four babies and then she found him dead in their new garage. You know, Paul Gray."

"Oh, yeah." Jenks immediately swallowed hard and looked away from Zac. "No, wait, that's not the name."

"It's not?"

"No. I think maybe it's Capri—"

"You're right, it is," Zac said. "I just used Gray because that's how you knew him."

"I never knew him," Jenks protested.

Zac leaned in closer. "Let's pretend he brought something in here."

"To pawn?"

"Let's say he wanted to fence something."

"I don't fence. That's illegal."

"Maybe you knew where to send him."

"If he came in, which he didn't and if I were a crook, which I ain't, I might have sent him somewhere. So what?"

"Exactly."

"What else can I do for you?"

"You see, I don't work in Seattle anymore. I don't really care what you do or don't do. But my old partner, he's the kind who does care. He'd want to tear the place apart, look over your records, maybe close you down. He's a real by-the-book kind of guy.

"But you aren't," Jenks said, irony in his eyes.

"Not so much. So, was anyone with Capri?"

Jenks met Zac's gaze and held it unblinking for a minute, then finally looked around the shop as if to make sure they were alone. He said, "You mean standing there with him?"

"No. No, I mean just kind of around. Was there anyone like that?"

Another minute passed as the wheels turned in Jenks's white head. "Maybe," he finally said.

"And this person seemed interested in Capri?"

Another minute passed as Jenks stared down into a glass case of estate jewelry. He finally said, "He wasn't advertising he was here, but I seen him lurking around and when Capri left, he followed him."

Zac traced a circle in the dust with his finger as he said, "Would you say he was the nervous type?"

"Jumpy. But I don't think Capri had the slightest idea he had a tail."

"At least not until it was too late," Zac said. "Now tell me what Capri brought in."

"I'M SORRY, Ms. Hart," the appraiser said as he turned a figurine over in his hands. His eyes were still watering—closing the basement window apparently hadn't helped with his allergies. He used a jeweler's loupe to study the mark on the bottom, which he'd uncovered by using a solvent to remove the felt pad. This time the mark was blue and encircled a large hole in the bottom. The appraiser sniffed and snorted as his allergies made him miserable.

The figurine itself was of a woman with red hair piled on her head, wearing a flowing yellow gown with a white frill. Brad Makko watched the appraiser with anxious eyes.

"This one is worth maybe five hundred dollars," the appraiser said at last. "The brunette wearing white and carrying the flowers, maybe she's a thousand, the others, much less."

Olivia sighed.

Brad Makko picked up the brunette in the white dress. "Mother loved these. I remember walking into her room one time and finding her talking to them as though they were real. I had no idea they had actual intrinsic value."

"I changed my mind," Olivia said. "You or your brother's wife should have them."

"But you wanted them for Danny's daughters."

"No. I'll pack them up for you. I'd just like to keep one of them." If each figurine was worth an average of five hundred dollars, it amounted to a sizeable chunk of change.

He smiled. "I guess I'm more sentimental than I thought. Thank you."

At that moment, Mr. Lawrence, in the act of setting the redhead figurine down in front of Olivia, sneezed several times in a row. Big, violent sneezes that racked his frame. The attack caught him so off guard he appeared to misjudge the distance and almost slammed the small sculpture onto the low table top. All three of them heard a cracking noise and watched as the statuette fell into four or five pieces.

Their collective gasp was followed by Lawrence apologizing fiercely as he mopped his nose. "I'll pay for it, of course. I can't believe—"

But Olivia was caught by what she saw laying in among the shattered china. Lawrence, following her gaze, abruptly stopped talking. Makko's intake of breath seemed to suck all the oxygen out of the room.

"What's that?" Olivia said.

She was staring at a red stone with such depth and clarity and sparkle it took her breath away. It was multifaceted and was easily an inch long, cut in a pear shape.

"Oh, my goodness," Lawrence said, his voice a good octave higher than it had been before. He sneezed again and hardly seemed to notice. "Do you know what that is?"

"A ruby?" Olivia said.

"No. That's a red diamond. There's only one like that in the world. That's the Debussy diamond."

"I don't—"

"The Debussy diamond. Stolen from a vault during a break-in a year or two ago. It was set in a broach back then. Diamonds and three sapphires, I believe. Two cops were killed during the escape. Other things were stolen, too. Let me think. Some kind of antiquity."

"I remember it now," Brad Makko said, his eyes still glued to the glittering bauble Lawrence had picked up to examine with his loupe. It appeared to be solidly attached to a concave piece of the porcelain, a piece that had once been part of the hoop skirt. "They never found out who did it."

"No," Lawrence muttered. The appraiser exerted a little pressure and the diamond came free. "Someone glued it up inside the figurine. "They must have chosen this one because the hole in the bottom was so big."

Meanwhile, Olivia picked up another piece of broken china and turned it over. It glittered with sparkling stones, all glued in place.

Brad said, "How did my brother end up with the Debussy diamond to say nothing of these other gemstones?"

"That's a very good question," Mr. Lawrence said.

"I just can't believe your brother would be involved with murder," Olivia said, her heart sinking. Her babies' father was a cold-blooded killer?

Brad cleared his throat. "I never thought much about it until now, but that theft went down in Vegas and it happened while Danny was visiting. I know there was one night when he got back late, looking real upset. Good lord, he left the next day."

"So, maybe the figurine wasn't broken during the break-in at my house," Olivia said, looking at Brad. "I bet your brother broke one the first time he was in debt, and then the day he was murdered, he was going to break another but was interrupted."

"I can't believe my little brother would be involved in murder."

"He'd have more trouble fencing the Debussy Diamond," the appraiser said. "That would take a special kind of buyer who didn't mind the blood that came with the stone. Now it can go back to its rightful owners."

"You take it," Olivia told the appraiser.

He put his equipment back into his briefcase and held up both hands. "No way," he said, and then sneezed three more times. "That's stolen property," he added as he dabbed at his watery eyes. "You need to call the police. These other figurines could be loaded with stones, too. Put them all somewhere safe."

"My thoughts exactly," Olivia said, carefully piling the diamonds and figurines back into the box. "Will you two gentlemen come with me?"

The men got up and followed her up the stairs. She led them up the next flight to the turret room where she opened the safe, tucked the statuettes and gems safely inside and closed the door, twirling the combination lock shut as the doorbell rang down below.

Olivia stood abruptly. "I have to get back to my children," she said, hoping that was Zac at the door.

Mr. Lawrence sneezed again. Sounding even more nasal than before, he said, "And I've got to get out of this neighborhood." They all went back downstairs to find a new contingent of willing hands, fussy babies and a noise level on the rise. No Zac.

Mr. Lawrence bade a hasty farewell as Sandy handed Jillian to Brad Makko along with a spit-up rag. "She's clean but hungry, just keep her occupied for a while, will you please?"

Brad took the baby with a big smile and, gently jouncing her in his arms, made his way toward the nursery. Half the women moved into the nursery behind him to start changing diapers while the other half scooted into the kitchen to make formula. Olivia promised Sandy she'd be right back, grabbed her phone and escaped out the back door where it was quiet enough to place a phone call to Zac.

Between the call from the gambler earlier that day and the discovery in the figurines, there was a lot to explain.

Zac met Dilly at the hospital and as they walked through the building, Dilly brought Zac up to speed on the investigation.

"I took Kellerman off the Hart house after your call," the wiry deputy reported.

"That's good. We can use him out near the highway. How about our star prisoner?"

"Twitch is talking to his lawyer. His car is clean,

by the way. No trace of a hit-and-run. On the other hand, the gun he fired last night is the same gun that fired the bullet that killed Danny Makko. He's still wearing the same shoes, too, and they match the imprint. The left-front tire on his car matches the mold we made out at the point. We don't have lab results back yet though we do know he's the same blood type as the second set of spatters at Olivia's house, but you can bet he's the murderer, all right."

"Turn off your phone," Zac cautioned as they entered the elevator. As he did the same, he added, "The staff at the hotel noticed someone matching Twitch's description hanging around when Danny Makko checked out. I think he knew Makko had fenced something before because he'd been hanging around Barry Pike and his minions. When he found out Makko was going to do it again, he must have followed Danny back here and the rest of it went down pretty much like we figured."

"Makes sense."

"He was fencing jewels. Good ones, according to my source."

"I wonder where he got those."

"The big question is was he working alone or with someone else? If he was, I'm betting his lawyer will encourage him to cut a deal, then maybe he'll talk."

They got off the elevator to find Zac's father

walking down the hall toward them, head bent, shoulders hunched, Olivia's mother walking beside him. Zac's heart seemed to shrink and go into hiding at the sight of them. "Faith," he whispered.

Gus Bishop looked up.

Juliet Hart said, "Don't worry, she's the same, Zac. In fact, her temperature has come down some. Your dad is just exhausted. He didn't stay away for more than four hours. I'm taking him downstairs for a cup of coffee. Sandy is coming over to take my place with Faith."

All of a sudden, Zac's earlier idea to disenfranchise himself from Olivia showed itself as the sorry excuse for a plan it was. His family and hers were too deeply intertwined. "I don't know how to thank you—"

"Faith is like a fifth daughter to me," Juliet said. "And you're like a son."

Zac hugged both older people. He stared long and hard into his dad's eyes and saw fatigue, but he also saw strength.

"Have you heard from Olivia today? I think she got an upsetting call this morning."

"Haven't heard a thing. Sandy will know."

As Juliet and Gus got into the elevator, Zac and Dilly went into Faith's room. If anything, Zac thought his sister looked worse than she had that morning. She was as pale as the little statue Olivia had left by her bed. Her bruises were dark, her healing abrasions garish against the snow-white of her skin. He took her hand and talked to her while Dilly shifted around uncomfortably. When the nurses came to do their routine checkups, he excused himself and walked Dilly back out into the parking lot. It was obvious his detective would rather be anywhere than at a hospital and Zac didn't blame him.

They both had calls waiting for them on their phones. Dilly sat in his patrol car to return his, Zac walked out into the parking lot, stretching his legs, to call Olivia. Sandy drove by while the phone rang and they exchanged waves.

"I hear you got a call from your gambler friend," Zac said when he heard Olivia's voice.

"I hung up on him. He made me mad."

Zac's lips twitched. He loved it when her temper got the better of her. The grin faded as he realized her quirks were not his concern. "Well, he's in jail now. So are the other two. And the man who killed Danny Makko is also in jail."

"The man from last night?"

"Yes."

"How is Faith? I called earlier—"

"She's the same. Your Mom is still here, I think more for Dad's sake than Faith's. I just saw Sandy arrive, too."

"She wanted to see if she could help. Zac, do you think the man you have in custody is the man who ran down Faith?"

Zac studied a crack in the pavement for a second. "You know, I don't. They found no traces of blood or anything else on his car and this is a guy who was wearing the same shoes as on the night he committed the murder. In other words, not the kind to have a second car at home to switch over to though we'll check to make sure. But something doesn't feel right about that."

She was quiet as she apparently assimilated all this. He marveled they could hold such a detached conversation and patted himself on the back. He was actually letting her go, just as he'd said he would. In some odd way, he was proud of himself.

She finally said, "Things are really chaotic here right now. It seems two groups of helpers got their wires crossed and both came. No one wanted to leave, so it's turned into a free for all. Brad Makko is hanging in there, bless his heart, but I have some really big news for you. Get this, we found the Debussy Diamond inside one of Danny's mother's figurines. Plus a lot of other really nice stones."

So that's where the jewels had come from. He said, "What's the Debussy Diamond?"

"I'll explain it later. The bad part of this is that

during the theft of the diamonds, there was a double murder and it looks like Danny was involved."

He stared at the faded yellow parking spot lines and frowned. "I'll come over."

"Good. I'm a little uncomfortable with all this loot in my office safe. Oh, I should tell you the figurine I set by Faith's bed might be full of stones, too. There's no way to know for sure, we haven't had time to investigate the others."

"I'll go grab it."

"No," she said immediately. "No, just leave it there, please. We can get it after she wakes up, okay?"

"Sure."

He started to click off, but then he heard her lower her voice. "Zac, are you still there?"

"Yeah, I'm here."

"Zac, I'm sorry."

He said nothing. What could he say?

"I botched things," she added. "Of course I know the difference between a man like Danny Makko and a man like Zac Bishop."

"Olivia, this is water under the bridge."

"I just wish so much I'd given myself time to think. Is it too late, Zac?"

"Too late for what?" he heard himself say.

"I see," she murmured. Her voice sounded hurt,

and though he wasn't proud of it, it almost made him feel good. Let her see how she liked it.

"I'll see you soon," he said, and listened as she disconnected.

As he folded the phone closed, the old throbbing ache in his heart started back up. His emotions were all over the map, bouncing around from ashamed to annoyed to vengeful. Not admirable. This woman could tie him up in knots with a casual toss of her head. He resented the power she had over him. It sounded as though she might be willing to reexamine the idea of a romance with him—was he up to the challenge?

He started retracing his steps across the parking lot, kicking a small stone in front of him, hands shoved in pockets, looking up when he heard a car door slam.

Dilly was charging toward him, the expression on his thin face somewhere between excited and stunned. While still eight feet away, Dilly started talking loud and fast. "You're not going to believe this. I was trying to get a make on Lindy Makko and then the Feds were using Danny Makko's fingerprints—"

"Just tell me what I'm not going to believe," Zac growled.

"I couldn't find a Lindy Makko anywhere, you know that, no one could. I decided to talk to Brad's wife since I haven't had a chance to track down Brad. I thought maybe she could give me more leads."

"And—" Zac prompted.

"No one answered the phone so I left a message. I just got a call back. But not from Maria, from Brad Makko. From Vegas."

"No, you couldn't find him because he's over at Olivia's house—"

"No, he's not. Brad Makko is in Vegas with his wife, Maria. He had a brother named Danny who died about five years ago. He and the wife were up in Canada visiting relatives but the relatives got sick so they came back early. He's never heard of Lindy Makko and get this, while they were gone someone broke into their house and stole a few papers including his driver's license. He doesn't drive anymore because of developing cataracts."

"Then who's at Olivia's house?" Zac said, muscles tightening.

"I don't know."

"Damn!"

"Wait, there's more. Hoopes heard back from the Feds. Using the fingerprints we sent, they got a positive ID on our dead man. His real name is Logan Cooke from Nebraska, an only child, family gone except for a wife named Shelby who is hopping mad because he stole her inheritance and blew town five years ago. Multiple arrests, federal charges for impersonating a US Marshal. Bank fraud. Conspiracy. He went to school at Harvard with Anthony Capri, who died right after graduation. In this latest version of his, he stole his old classmate's identity—"

Zac had stopped listening. He had his cell phone out in a flash and pushed the button to connect him to Olivia as he ran the distance to his own car.

She didn't answer.

Chapter Twelve

Olivia turned off her phone, stuck it in her pocket and stood outside, taking deep breaths of warm air tainted with the tang of nearby Puget Sound. The late afternoon skies were growing increasingly dark and cloudy, the wind rustling the maple tree boughs. She recalled hearing rain was predicted before nightfall.

So what if Zac had given up on her? she asked herself as she studied a redwood planter that was in sore need of weeding. She was the sole provider for her babies, worried sick about Faith and in possession of a few million dollars worth of stolen diamonds. She had to call her lawyer and find out if she was indebted to Danny's creditors seeing as she'd never been his legal wife. The other three babies had appointments tomorrow at the pediatrician's office, her house was as busy as an airport before Thanksgiving.

She couldn't allow herself to get sidetracked by love.

The word stopped her dead in her tracks.

Love?

For Zac?

For a second, her mind replayed a montage of moments. Zac presenting her with four pink roses in the hospital, Zac's hands steadying her outrage when the man she thought she'd married turned out to be a fraud, Zac's arms absorbing the shock of finding her pretend husband buried in the garage.

His lips, the way he looked at her, the want and need she'd been sensing and responding to but had been afraid to return. When he'd pushed her toward acknowledging her feelings, she'd turned into a yellow-bellied coward. She hadn't even let him utter the damning words she no longer trusted: *I love you*.

But she did believe in those words. It wasn't Zac's fault she'd put blind faith in them once before. Zac wasn't the man she would always think of as Anthony.

She continued up the back steps and into the kitchen. The room was a giant mess, the remnants of a late lunch fixed for all the helpers covering every surface. The muted sounds of voices, laughter and the occasional newborn gurgle filtering in from the rest of the house comforted her.

The phone rang not a foot from where she stood. She didn't want to answer it, afraid it might be Zac. It stopped ringing and a second later, Tabitha called her name. "Olivia? Phone. It's Zac."

Olivia went through the kitchen door into the living room. "Tell him I'm busy right now," she said, "I'll talk to him when he gets here."

As Tabitha communicated her message, Olivia entered the nursery. Megan was sitting in the rocker with Brianna, singing to her. Lori and Paty had apparently given Jillian a bath and were in the process of patting her dry, giggling at the baby's funny faces. "Keep her warm," Olivia cautioned, stopping to cover her baby. She deeply appreciated all the help, she knew she needed it, but sometimes the place was like a zoo and she felt left out.

"Where are Antoinette and Juliet?" she asked no one in particular.

"Brad still has Antoinette," Megan said. "He's been walking her all over the place, trying to settle her down."

"The ladies from the bowling league are bathing Juliet," Lori said. "Don't look so alarmed, Sandy taught them how to do it before she left."

The bath station was set up in the small room across the hall from the bathroom. Olivia made her way to this room, expecting to run into Brad Makko.

She found three of the bowling-league ladies very gently giving Juliet a sponge bath, doing it like pros.

Olivia once again looked around for Brad. "If you guys are about done," she said, "I'll go get Antoinette and bathe her next."

"We can do it."

"No," Olivia said, kissing Juliet's tummy. "I want to do it myself."

"Give us a few moments."

Tabitha met her in the hall. "Zac says he has to talk to you now," she said. "I tried to get him to tell me what's so important, but he's so stubborn…"

"Okay. Where are Brad and Antoinette?"

"I don't know. I haven't seen them since I got home from school."

"Go check the basement for me, will you?"

With a roll of the eyes, Tabitha went off down the stairs as Olivia ducked into the living room and picked up the receiver. "Hello?" she said, distracted as Tabitha came bounding back up the stairs, shaking her head. Olivia pointed up the stairs to the turret room and Tabitha kept climbing.

"Where's Brad Makko?" Zac said. His voice held an ominous tone she'd never heard before.

"I'm not sure."

"Listen to me. Under no circumstances should you leave him alone with any of the babies, okay?"

"You're frightening me," she said as Tabitha came down the stairs, shrugging. "Why shouldn't he—"

"Please, Olivia."

"He was comforting Antoinette," she said. "I can't find her or him." Covering the mouthpiece, she looked at Tabitha. "Check the front yard. Maybe he took her outside."

As Tabitha opened the front door, Olivia turned back to the phone. "What's going on, Zac?"

"Is Makko out front? I'm about a block from you now."

Tabitha came back inside. "His car is gone," she said.

"He's gone," Olivia said in wonder. "Where did he go, what's happening? Where's Antoinette?"

"Zac just drove up," Tabitha announced, her voice reflecting Olivia's anxiety.

Olivia dropped the phone and ran to front door. Zac had jumped out of his car almost before it stopped moving. Their gazes collided as they ran toward one another.

A THOROUGH SEARCH of the house revealed the unmistakable fact that the man masquerading as Brad Makko was gone and had apparently taken Antoinette with him. Pale and trembling, Olivia walked from room to room as if unable to accept what was happening. Zac dogged her heels, explaining what Dilly had uncovered just minutes before.

"So he wasn't Danny's brother," she said, finally stopping and leaning against the wall for support. They were standing in front of the basement stairs. Zac had assigned two adults to each remaining child and told them not to let their charge out of their sight.

When everyone stopped to think about it, they agreed that Brad had hung around the nursery for quite a while before finally disappearing down the hall. No one could recall how long it had been since they'd seen him, only that it could have been up to a half hour. Zac had immediately put a tap on Olivia's line and instigated a search. There wasn't much to do now but wait.

"There is no Danny Makko. His name was Logan Cooke."

"And you don't know who pretended to be Brad Makko?"

"Not yet. Only that he checked out of the hotel this morning. Dilly is over there getting fingerprints. Unless the maid was very thorough, we'll know shortly."

"Why would he take a five-pound infant? I don't understand—"

"It has to be tied in the jewels you discovered earlier. He and Logan Cooke must have been partners.

If I had to hazard a guess, I'd say Logan ran out on his partner and disappeared into Anthony Capri's identity."

"That's why Anthony didn't like photos being taken of him."

"It might explain who burned down the wedding photographer's shop, too. Anyway, when you gave birth to the quads, your mother held up Logan's photo for one and all to see. The man masquerading as Brad Makko must have seen the newscast and realized where his two-timing cohort had resettled."

"He got here after the murder but in time to get in on all the confusion and tension. Earlier today he asked me about Vegas," she added. "He asked if Danny had ever talked about him and the parties they attended."

"The jewels were stolen during a party at a private residence."

"But why would this man take Antoinette—"

The phone rang and she froze.

Zac had previously propped open the kitchen door. He dashed in there now. "We'll pick up at the same time," he said, hand poised over the receiver in the kitchen. "If it's him, try to keep him on the line."

With a nod, they picked up the phone.

"YOU KNOW WHAT I HAVE?" the man Olivia had known as Brad Makko said.

Olivia closed her eyes. She could hear frantic cries in the background. Her breasts tingled at the sound, a primal response to the stimulus. Her baby needed her. Olivia's insides seemed to collapse. "Bring her back," she said as tears rolled down her cheeks.

He spoke very fast. "Get together all five dolls and the diamonds. Grab that bell thing. Get in your car, take your cell phone, start driving. Give me the number. I'll call with directions. Start now."

From the kitchen, Zac vigorously shook his head no.

Olivia rattled off her cell number then said, "I can't start now."

"Why?"

"Because my sister took my car to the hotel to look for you."

"Why would she do that?"

"We were desperate," Olivia said, her gaze fastened to Zac's. "I…she had to do something."

"Take your mother's car—"

"She's still at the hospital."

"Then get a damn taxi," he shouted.

"My sister will be back in a few minutes. I'll do what you say, just give me a little more time."

"You have thirty minutes. Do this alone or you'll never see this baby again."

The phone went dead. Zac was at her side almost immediately. She turned to him, eyes flashing, fists clenched. "Why did I just subject my baby to thirty more minutes with that madman? She needs me now. I should have done what he said."

He grabbed her arms and stared hard into her eyes. "Do you trust me, Olivia?"

"Yes. Of course I trust you."

"You know I care deeply for you and your daughters and would never jeopardize any of you?"

"Yes," she said, the shakes coming back. His eyes were so blue, so intense. "Why? What are you saying?"

"I'm saying we can't do things his way. We can't trust him."

"But—"

"He's going to need to get away after you give him what he wants. He's going to know every law officer in the state is on his tail. He's going to want insurance."

"Antoinette!"

"Yes."

She tore herself away, unable to stand inactivity, pacing back and forth, straining for glimpses of the other babies safely ensconced in loving arms, knowing she would die if anything happened to any of them.

"Where do you take such a tiny baby?" Zac asked.

"What do you mean?"

"I mean that this guy hardly looks like the kind of man to be in charge of such a small infant. He'd stand out in a store or restaurant, we've got cops combing the streets and hotels. I bet half of Westerly already knows the baby has been taken. He can't be too far away because he's got to meet you somewhere."

"He could be on the Interstate by now."

"The Washington Highway Patrol are looking for him. The FBI was alerted there's been a kidnapping, he's not going to drive around for an hour."

"Maybe he drove out in the woods and is sitting in his car—" Olivia stopped talking as she thought of Antoinette in a car with that man. The rain had started several minutes ago and the temperature had dropped. The last anyone saw of Antoinette, she'd been wearing a diaper and a onesie and had been wrapped in a receiving blanket. Unless Makko or whatever his name was had planned this abduction, and she didn't think he had, the baby wasn't clothed for the cold nor was she secured in a car seat or even a bassinette.

"I heard Antoinette cry in the background," Zac

said. "It didn't sound like it came from the inside of a car."

"The new house," Olivia said. "I bet he took her out to the house on the point. He mentioned he'd gone there this morning. We talked about how it was abandoned."

Megan came down the stairs with a box in which she'd placed the figurines from the safe. Tabitha brought in the plaster bell from the nursery.

Zac's cell rang. He mostly listened to his caller, then hung up. "That was Hoopes. The abductor's name is Richard Deerfield. He's a thief, working out of Vegas. The Vegas police tried to tie him in with the Debussy robbery two years ago but didn't have enough to hold him on."

"So he sees us uncover the diamonds and then lock them away. But why that ugly bell, why does he want that? It's not his mother's because everything he told me is a lie. There is no mother who collected figurines."

Zac shrugged. "Maybe the big glassy-looking things are real stones. Who cares?" Zac stuck it in the box.

"Maybe the whole wife thing was a lie, too—"

"No, that was true, he just made up a name. There is a wife, back in Nebraska, I think."

"Good," Olivia said with feeling as Zac picked up the box.

"If you think you're going out there without me, you're nuts," she said.

"This is a two-man operation. I'll get Dilly—"

"No you won't. I'm your ticket into that house. If he sees me arrive alone with a box, he's going to let me in. If he sees any of you or the FBI, he might put up a fight and Antoinette could get caught in the crosshairs." She took the box from his arms. "I'm coming."

ZAC INSISTED ON BACKUP and for that Olivia couldn't blame him. They took her car and met Hoopes and Dilly out near the spot where the driveway took off from the main road. Deputy Kellerman stayed at Olivia's house with everyone except the people still at the hospital with Faith.

Zac had spent the drive wrapping his gun in a watertight plastic bag he'd taken from Olivia's kitchen drawers while she packed warmer clothes for Antoinette.

They stood together in the last of the daylight, huddled between the two vehicles, Olivia under an umbrella, Dilly and Hoopes in rain hats, Zac bareheaded and apparently oblivious to the pouring rain. He still wore the clothes he'd worn to court, only he'd left the jacket in the car and taken off the tie. The rain soaked his shirt, plastering it to his broad shoulders and lean frame and despite everything Olivia found courage at the way he assumed control.

"What's the plan?" Dilly asked.

"You two are staying out here by the road," Zac said. "It's your responsibility to make sure Deerfield doesn't get past you."

"What if he leaves by boat?"

"I don't think he's had time to arrange for a boat. He isn't expecting us. Hell, let's be honest, we don't even know for sure he's in there. I'll ride most of the way with Olivia, but I'll get out of the car before the last couple of turns. She'll proceed to the house by herself."

"You're giving him another hostage," Dilly said, frowning.

Olivia chimed in. "I have to get to Antoinette no matter what. If he takes her away without me, she's in horrible danger."

"He's not taking either one of you anywhere," Zac said very quietly. He glanced at his watch. "We'd better get going."

As Hoopes and Dilly got into their unit to move it, Zac hunkered down on the passenger side of Olivia's car and she slid behind the wheel. She glanced at Zac who winked at her in the fading light. "Don't turn on your headlights," he cautioned as they entered the gloom of the woods.

She drove carefully until he touched her leg

"Stop up here and I'll get out of the car. You wait for five minutes and then proceed. Don't worry about me, just take care of Antoinette. Try to give me a little time to set things in motion."

"What things?"

He smiled. "Hell, I don't know. I'm hoping something comes to me."

"Okay." Her hands began trembling and she forced herself to steady them. She stopped the car in the middle of the road and looked again at Zac. His gaze seemed to burn itself into her head.

"Zac, I—"

"Olivia, damn it all, I have to say this. I love you. I have for years. That's why I was such a jerk when you got married, that's why I can't just be your buddy anymore. I want you as my lover, as my wife, I won't settle for anything else. I'm going to stop Deerfield and make sure you and the babies are safe and then be warned, I'm launching an all-out attack to win your heart." He leaned across the seat, pulled her into his arms and crushed his lips against hers.

Before she could respond, he'd opened the door and fled into the trees.

ZAC RAN perpendicular to the road, headed for the water. The land around the house had been cleared and as such was way too open for a frontal attack.

He'd have to go by water, from the point of land closest to the house but not within view.

He skirted the north side of the point until he came to a spot several hundred feet away where the trees grew right to the edge of the shore offering maximum cover. He could see a dim light in the house jutting out over the water—so they were right, Deerfield was hiding Antoinette in the house her father had built.

Zac stuffed the plastic-wrapped revolver in the waistband of his slacks. On subsequent forays to the house while investigating the murder, he'd noticed a dock out in back and he could see it there now with a covered ramp leading up to the deck. As it was low tide, the ramp was steeply tilted. Girding himself for the shock, he waded in. The relentless rain fell like darts, the water froze everything it touched as it inched up his body.

He was going to need more than his share of luck to live through this.

OLIVIA PULLED into the clearing, relieved to see the small white rental last spotted in front of her house. She got out of the car, walked to the trunk and took out the box.

"That's far enough," Deerfield said from the porch. She hadn't noticed him in the shadows, but, of course, he'd probably heard her approaching vehicle.

"Where is she?" Olivia said, ignoring his warning and walking toward the house, legs stiff, feet numb, straining for sounds that would tell her Antoinette was alive, that Zac was near—

He lowered a gun at her. The benign uncle expression was gone. She now saw any resemblance to the man he'd claimed to be his brother was all on the surface, a matter of coloring and size only.

And yet at one time he'd seemed familiar. As he moved across the porch in the failing light, dressed in a long jacket, she knew she'd seen him somewhere before he introduced himself as her supposed brother-in-law. Where?

"Your kid is inside," he said. "She cried herself to sleep. How did you figure out I was here?"

"You talked about this place this morning. Listen, I brought the stuff you want. I don't care what you do with it. Give me my daughter and we'll call it good."

He cocked the gun. The menacing click seemed to echo in the rain. "Take off your coat and throw it over here."

"There's something in—"

"Shut up and do as you're told."

She took off the coat, shivering as the cold drops pelted her head and shoulders, and threw it to him.

He immediately noticed the weight in the left pocket and glanced at her sharply as he fumbled to find out what it was.

"It's a bottle for the baby," she said. "I have a diaper bag in the car with warm clothes—"

"Shut up," he repeated. He motioned her up onto the porch under the overhang.

"Put the box down, face the house and spread-eagle."

Once again she did as he asked without question, just anxious for him to realize she wasn't armed so he'd let her in to get Antoinette. The frisk was clumsy but impersonal.

"Turn around," he said, and threw the coat at her.

"I want my child," she said as she put the coat back on.

"Where's the boyfriend?"

"You mean Sheriff Bishop? Do you think I would risk my baby by bringing a cop with me?"

He answered by raising the gun to her head and grabbing her arm. He marched her back to the car which he searched by sight, including the trunk, then he forced her to accompany him as they rounded the house, him darting glances into the forest or out over the darkening water, Olivia peering desperately through her wet hair into each window they passed, straining for a glimpse of her baby.

A light shone through the window in the back and she desperately struggled to see inside the lit room as Deerfield stared out at the water. She caught a glimpse of a small hand. Antoinette! The hand was so utterly still Olivia's heart froze, then the tiny fingers fluttered. Olivia almost fell to her knees with relief. Deerfield pulled her along and as they finished circling the deck, she wondered if he'd seen some sign of Zac and if he had if he was planning to ambush him. She had to save Antoinette and she had to save Zac. There was no either-or. Both.

But he kept moving. By the time they got back to the box, he seemed more relaxed and his greedy eyes scanned the contents. "Is it all there?"

"Except one figurine. I didn't have time to go get it."

"I knew Logan's mother was dead, so I figured the dolls were a hiding place for what was left of the gemstones. You could have saved us all a lot of trouble if you'd put those dolls and that bell down in the basement in Logan's boxes right from the start."

She was not only anxious to delay him in case Zac needed time to implement whatever plan he might have come up with, she was also curious as hell. She said, "Why in the world do you want that ugly bell?"

"Pick up that rock," he said, pointing the gun at

a rock by the bottom step, then quickly aiming it back at her.

She darted down the steps and picked up the rock, glad to get back under cover. "Now whack the rim of the bell," he said. "Not too hard, just enough to crack the plaster."

Kneeling, Olivia turned the bell and smashed the rock against the rim.

"Harder," he said.

She used more force. The third time worked. A big piece of plaster sloughed off revealing a rich gold sculptured surface underneath.

"I knew it!" Deerfield said, moving around the box to get a better look.

"What is it?"

"It's a vase dating back to before Christ. It was in the safe with the Debussy Diamond. Logan must have disguised it as a bell by covering it with that goop and turning it upside down. The minute I looked in that nursery today and saw it, I knew what it was. I have a buyer, it's worth a fortune. Now, smash the rest of the dolls. Hurry."

One by one she did as he asked. Two had stones glued inside, one was empty. He told her to hand him the Debussy Diamond which he pocketed.

She'd watched him as he moved and now she said, "You were the one who attacked me in the basement the first night I was home."

"I heard you and the cop talking earlier about searching the boxes," he said. "I had to see if Logan had stashed the goods in an obvious place."

The wheels turned and clicked into place. Olivia said, "You were outside my house the night the gamblers came to threaten me. You were walking down the sidewalk and then you just disappeared. That's where I saw you before, why you seemed familiar."

He half smiled. "I knew you were expecting those bozos to do something nasty to someone you cared about, so I followed the cop's sister home and ran her down when she stopped at the old man's house. I'm just not into knives, too messy. All I wanted to do was confuse the issue, add pressure."

"You ran over Faith! But your car is a little white rental—"

"My car is a black sedan with Vegas plates currently parked at Sea Tac long-term parking where I stashed it after hitting the girl. I rented this one and then showed up at your place. Pretty clever, if I do say so myself."

"You might have killed her."

"In case you haven't been listening, honey, I've already killed two cops."

"Then Logan didn't shoot anyone during the robbery?"

"All Logan Cooke did was grease his way into the

party and disable the alarm. Don't look too hopeful, just about everything I told you about him is true. Don't waste any tears over that jerk. After the theft I made the big mistake of letting him talk me into holding on to the loot until things calmed down. He ran out on me. I should have known better than to trust him."

"And the photographs you showed me?"

Deerfield scanned the yard as he said, "None of the photos were really Logan besides the graduation and college pics I took off an Internet site and the one of him and me in Vegas."

Through the open door behind him, Olivia heard Antoinette cry as though startled from sleep. Once again, her insides jolted in response. Ignoring the black muzzle pointed at her heart, she rushed past Deerfield and into the much darker house, following the cries through the open walls where a light made a small oasis in the farthest corner. She heard Deerfield's pounding footsteps behind her.

Her tiny daughter lay on a man's flannel shirt on the floor in the darkest shadows cast by the towering stack of unopened baby things Olivia had ordered online. For a second it stunned Olivia the boxes were still there, but it had only been a few days, not the months it seemed. There hadn't been time to send things back.

Antoinette had kicked off a man's sweater that

had been used as a cover. Her arms were spread out to her sides, her knees drawn up to her chest, her eyes closed, her mouth open. She was crying so hard she was momentarily unable to catch her breath. Olivia immediately picked her up and tucking her beneath her coat, held her tightly against the warmth of her own body. The baby exhaled with a sob. Olivia whirled to face Deerfield who ground to a stop at the doorway of the framed room.

"Make her stop," he said.

"I'm trying," Olivia said as the baby continued to wail. "She's cold and hungry. If I could give her the bottle—"

"We don't have time for that. You're driving. We're going on a little trip."

The thought of getting in a car with Deerfield suddenly seemed like the worst idea in the world. If she only knew where Zac was. That thought was immediately followed by another—she couldn't depend solely on Zac to get them out of this mess. She had to use her own head and take any opportunity that presented itself.

She took a few steps toward Deerfield who was apparently so certain she would meekly obey that he turned his back to her. In that instant, she stepped quickly to her right, behind some of the boxes. He must have sensed her movement. He yelled at her, but she kept circling. She didn't think he would risk wounding her or the baby, they were both too valuable as hostages.

She was wrong. A bullet cracked behind her, glass shattered to her left. He'd shot out one of the French doors. She tried to knock a big box off the stack in her wake. The twisting motion seemed to rip her abdomen apart and she gasped in pain, but she kept going toward the French doors. Splintered wood ripped at her coat as she maneuvered her way through the wrecked door and broke into the cold outside air.

The decks were covered and protected from rain. They were also darkly shadowed and she wasn't familiar with them. She just knew they changed levels over and over again. She stayed close to the side of the house, feeling her way, the drumming of rain on the roof echoing the hammering of her heart.

Deerfield crashed through the door behind her, holding the electric lantern aloft, the light swaying to and fro. She tried to shrink, but of course, Antoinette's cries made them sitting ducks. Deerfield immediately zeroed in on them and laughed. It was not a pleasant sound.

"You bitch," he said. "You didn't accomplish a damn thing." He approached with heavy, determined steps. He'd scratched himself coming through the door but seemed heedless of the red streaks blossoming across his face.

The light arced across the dry wood between them. Olivia stood mesmerized and then she finally noticed some of the wood decking was wet. It took less than a second for the explanation to hit her. She could even decipher a footprint. She looked up and met Deerfield's gaze. He immediately dropped his to examine what she'd seen and she knew it was only a matter of a heartbeat before he reached the same conclusion she had.

She sensed rather than saw a dark shape behind her. Holding on to Antoinette for all she was worth, Olivia turned her back to the side of the house and slid down the wall to a sitting position, cradling Antoinette between her chest and bent knees, oblivious to the pain this position created in her own body, anxious only to shield her tiny daughter from whatever came next.

Almost at once, gunfire exploded from everywhere, renting the night air until a dense and abiding silence fell like the closing curtain of an opera.

Almost as quickly, the quiet unraveled, revealing the steady beat of the rain on the roof, the baby's cries now little more than whimpers, the splashing of the water against the pier twenty feet away.

Shaking like a leaf, Olivia raised her head and slowly opened her eyes. Deerfield's body lay in a bloody heap. The lantern had landed on its side and cast macabre shadows on the deck and house. She looked the other direction into the dark. Nothing.

Where was Zac? Had he been hit? Catching a sob in the back of her throat, she held the baby tight and started to get up. She had to find him and help him—

He staggered at last from the gloom and collapsed next to her, his gun still in his hand. She heard the weapon clunk onto the deck as he set it aside.

"Are you okay?" he asked.

"Yes. Are you?"

"Yes. Antoinette?"

"She's okay, too."

He put an arm around Olivia's shoulders and ran his free hand over Antoinette's head. The baby grew very still as she turned her cheek toward his palm and seemed to gaze up at him.

The smile that curved his lips in response pierced Olivia's heart like a spear fashioned out of pure light.

"It's over," he said.

She leaned her head against his arm. He was icy cold and thoroughly drenched. His heartbeat was so strong it seemed to vibrate through his body and into hers.

How could she ever have resisted him? How could she not have seen, not have known what he meant to her, what he would mean to her children? It was as though she'd been blindfolded.

Well, the mask was off now and she could see very clearly and what she saw was her future all wrapped up in this one man. This time it was real, it wasn't an escape, it was a life. She was more than ready to open her heart, to fall in love for the first time.

"As soon as I catch my breath and thaw out a little, I'm going to launch Operation Make Olivia Love Me," he said as approaching sirens sounded from the driveway. His head thumped against the side of the house as he looked down at her. "Is that okay with you?"

She touched his face, then grasped his cold hand in hers, too choked with emotion to speak.

Luckily a kiss is worth a thousand words…

Epilogue

One month later

Zac carefully laid Juliet in her bassinette, hitched his hands on his waist and surveyed what had formally been his bedroom. It was now a nursery with four little bassinets and all the rest of the paraphernalia that comes along with four babies.

His babies.

His and Olivia's.

In a six-week span, he'd gone from a man in love with a married woman to a man married to the love of his life. From detective in Seattle to sheriff in Westerly. To incomplete and alone to surrounded by females, all of whom he loved more than life itself.

All and all, not bad.

"You look like a man afraid to move lest he wake a baby," Olivia said from the doorway.

He turned quickly and smiled at her. He hadn't

heard her come home. She looked beautiful in a soft green dress, her dark hair waving around her face.

Was she really his wife, was she really standing there looking at him with love and desire in her eyes?

"Well, as you know, it's no easy task getting them all down at the same time," he said as he walked to the doorway to join her. "How's Faith?"

"She's doing better," Olivia said as she wrapped her arms around him. "She hopes to get out of rehab in a few days. Her limp is better."

"That's great. And what did the lawyer say?"

"Long or short version?"

"Short." He let his eyes and hands wander across her clothes, lingering near the buttons over her breasts. Nuzzling her neck, he whispered, "Really short."

He lifted her into his arms and she laughed softly, a throaty sound that enflamed him. As he carried her down the hall toward their room, she said, "I don't owe anyone anything. As you know, I sold the car and sent the proceeds from the sale and the ring to Logan Cooke's wife. Oh, and the lawyer informed me that Grant and Hugh Robinson paid my hospital bills. Can you believe that?"

"Good for them," Zac said as he maneuvered them through the narrow doorway.

He set her down on the bed and lowered himself atop her. He planned to take his time undressing her, planned to spend the next hour or two reminding her in every way imaginable that he couldn't live without her, that she was the center of his universe.

"I love you so much," she whispered against his ear.

"Talk is cheap, babe, show me," he murmured, sliding onto the bed next to her, starting in on those flirty buttons.

"I'd be happy to show you," she said, smiling as she slid her fingers down his torso toward his belt buckle…

A soft cry floated down the hallway followed by another and another and yet another.

They looked at each other, smiling. Then they got to their feet, and arm in arm, went to tend to their babies.

* * * * *

Eight years ago Matt Shaffer had vanished out of Natalie Rothchild's life, leaving behind a one-line note tucked under a pillow that had grown cold: *I'm sorry, but this just isn't going to work.*

That was it. No explanation, no real indication of remorse. The note had been as clinical and compassionless as an eviction notice, which, in effect, it had been, Natalie thought as she navigated through the morning traffic. Matt had written the note to evict her from his life.

She'd spent the next two weeks crying, breaking down without warning as she walked down the street, or as she sat staring at a meal she couldn't bring herself to eat.

Candace, she remembered with a bittersweet pang, had tried to get her to go clubbing in order to get her to forget about Matt.

She'd turned her twin down, but she did get her act together. If Matt didn't think enough of their relationship to try to contact her, to try to make her understand why he'd changed so radically from lover to stranger, then to hell with him. He was dead to her, she resolved. And he'd remained that way.

Until twenty minutes ago.

The adrenaline in her veins kept mounting.

Natalie focused on her driving. Vegas in the daylight wasn't nearly as alluring, as magical and glitzy as it was after dark. Like an aging woman best seen in soft lighting, Vegas's imperfections were all visible in the daylight. Natalie supposed that was why people like her sister didn't like to get up until noon. They lived for the night.

Except that Candace could no longer do that.

The thought brought a fresh, sharp ache with it.

"Damn it, Candy, what a waste," Natalie murmured under her breath.

She pulled up before the Janus casino. One of the three valets currently on duty came to life and made a beeline for her vehicle.

"Welcome to the Janus," the young attendant said cheerfully as he opened her door with a flourish.

"We'll see," she replied solemnly.

As he pulled away with her car, Natalie looked up at the casino's logo. Janus was the Roman god with two faces, one pointed toward the past, the other facing the future. It struck her as rather ironic, given what she was doing here, seeking out someone from her past in order to get answers so that the future could be settled.

The moment she entered the casino, the Vegas phenomena took hold. It was like stepping into a world where time did not matter or even make an appearance. There was only a sense of "now."

Because in Natalie's experience she'd discovered that bartenders knew the inner workings of any establishment they worked for better than anyone else, she made her way to the first bar she saw within the casino.

The bartender in attendance was a gregarious man in his early forties. He had a quick, sexy smile, which was probably one of the main reasons he'd been hired. His name tag identified him as Kevin.

Moving to her end of the bar, Kevin asked, "What'll it be, pretty lady?"

"Information." She saw a dubious look cross his brow. To counter that, she took out her badge. Granted she wasn't here in an official capacity, but Kevin didn't need to know that. "Were you on duty last night?"

Kevin began to wipe the gleaming black surface of the bar. "You mean during the gala?"

"Yes."

The smile gracing his lips was a satisfied one. Last night had obviously been profitable for him, she judged. "I caught an extra shift."

She took out Candace's photograph and carefully placed it on the bar. "Did you happen to see this woman there?"

The bartender glanced at the picture. Mild interest turned to recognition. "You mean Candace Roth-child? Yeah, she was here, loud and brassy as always. But not for long," he added, looking rather disappointed. There was always a circus when Candace was around, Natalie thought. "She and the boss had at it and then he had our head of security escort her out."

She latched onto the first part of his statement. "They argued? About what?"

He shook his head. "Couldn't tell you. Too far away for anything but body language," he confessed.

"And the head of security?" she asked.

"He got her to leave."

She leaned in over the bar. "Tell me about him."

"Don't know much," the bartender admitted. "Just that his name's Matt Shaffer. Boss flew him in from L.A., where he was head of security for Montgomery Enterprises."

There was no avoiding it, she thought darkly. She was going to have to talk to Matt. The thought left her cold. "Do you know where I can find him right now?"

Kevin glanced at his watch. "He should be in his

office. On the second floor, toward the rear." He gave her the numbers of the rooms where the monitors that kept watch over the casino guests as they tried their luck against the house were located.

Taking out a twenty, she placed it on the bar. "Thanks for your help."

Kevin slipped the bill into his vest pocket. "Any time, lovely lady," he called after her. "Any time."

She debated going up the stairs, then decided on the elevator. The car that took her up to the second floor was empty. Natalie stepped out of the elevator, looked around to get her bearings and then walked toward the rear of the floor.

"Into the Valley of Death rode the six hundred," she silently recited, digging deep for a line from a poem by Tennyson. Wrapping her hand around a brass handle, she opened one of the glass doors and walked in.

The woman whose desk was closest to the door looked up. "You can't come in here. This is a restricted area."

Natalie already had her ID in her hand and held it up. "I'm looking for Matt Shaffer," she told the woman.

God, even saying his name made her mouth go dry. She was supposed to be over him, to have moved on with her life. What happened?

The woman began to answer her. "He's—"

"Right here."

The deep voice came from behind her. Natalie felt every single nerve ending go on tactical alert at the same moment that all the hairs at the back of her neck stood up. Eight years had passed, but she would have recognized his voice anywhere.

* * * * *

Why did Matt Shaffer leave heiress-turned-cop
Natalie Rothchild?
What does he know about the death of
Natalie's twin sister?
Come and meet these two reunited lovers and
learn the secrets of the Rothchild family in
THE HEIRESS'S 2-WEEK AFFAIR
by USA TODAY bestselling author
Marie Ferrarella.
The first book in
Silhouette® Romantic Suspense's
wildly romantic new continuity,
LOVE IN 60 SECONDS!
Available April 2009.

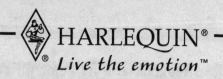

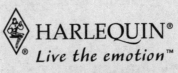

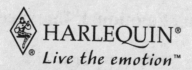

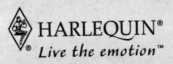

HARLEQUIN®
Presents®

The world's bestselling romance series...
The series that brings you your favorite authors,
month after month:

Helen Bianchin...Emma Darcy
Lynne Graham...Penny Jordan
Miranda Lee...Sandra Marton
Anne Mather...Carole Mortimer
Melanie Milburne...Michelle Reid

and many more talented authors!

Wealthy, powerful, gorgeous men...
Women who have feelings just like your own...
The stories you love, set in exotic, glamorous locations...

HARLEQUIN®
Presents®

Seduction and Passion Guaranteed!

HPDIR08

www.eHarlequin.com

Harlequin® Historical
Historical Romantic Adventure!

Imagine a time of chivalrous knights and unconventional ladies, roguish rakes and impetuous heiresses, rugged cowboys and spirited frontierswomen— these rich and vivid tales will capture your imagination!

Harlequin Historical . . . they're too good to miss!

HHDIR06